Cd⁹ 9-25-96

✓ S0-CAY-529

DUMB AND DUMBER

As Clint stepped outside he saw the man ahead of him crossing the street, still counting his money. From the shadows of an alley Clint saw three figures come into view.

The three dark figures descended on the man with raised arms, and Clint knew he had no time to reach them.

"Look out!" he shouted, but not quick enough. There was a thud as something hit the man, either on the shoulder or on the head.

Clint drew his gun. He didn't want to kill anyone, but he couldn't let the man be killed. Robbed, maybe, but not killed.

"Hold it!"

The three men turned and all went for their guns.

"Shit," Clint said, and fired.

DON'T MISS THESE
ALL-ACTION WESTERN SERIES
FROM THE BERKLEY PUBLISHING GROUP

THE GUNSMITH by J. R. Roberts
Clint Adams was a legend among lawmen, outlaws, and ladies. They called him . . . the Gunsmith.

LONGARM by Tabor Evans
The popular long-running series about U.S. Deputy Marshal Long—his life, his loves, his fight for justice.

SLOCUM by Jake Logan
Today's longest-running action Western. John Slocum rides a deadly trail of hot blood and cold steel.

THE GUNSMITH

177

BURIED PLEASURES

J. R. ROBERTS

JOVE BOOKS, NEW YORK

If you purchased this book without a cover, you should be aware that this book is stolen property. It was reported as "unsold and destroyed" to the publisher, and neither the author nor the publisher has received any payment for this "stripped book."

BURIED PLEASURES

A Jove Book / published by arrangement with
the author

PRINTING HISTORY
Jove edition / September 1996

All rights reserved.
Copyright © 1996 by Robert J. Randisi.
This book may not be reproduced in whole
or in part, by mimeograph or any other means,
without permission. For information address:
The Berkley Publishing Group, 200 Madison Avenue,
New York, New York 10016.

The Putnam Berkley World Wide Web site address is
http://www.berkley.com

ISBN: 0-515-11943-1

A JOVE BOOK®
Jove Books are published by The Berkley Publishing Group,
200 Madison Avenue, New York, New York 10016.
JOVE and the "J" design are trademarks
belonging to Jove Publications, Inc.

PRINTED IN THE UNITED STATES OF AMERICA

10 9 8 7 6 5 4 3 2 1

THE GUNSMITH

177

BURIED PLEASURES

PROLOGUE

Bill Benedict couldn't believe his luck. When he'd checked into the Barrows Boardinghouse he had admired the beauty of both mother and daughter. Admittedly, the mother was more his age—she was over forty and still lovely, while he was thirty-eight—but there was no doubt in his mind that the daughter had been giving him the eye all through dinner. The girl was probably all of nineteen or so, and so fresh that she made his teeth ache.

So the first piece of his luck was that she had taken a shine to him. Of that he was sure. His other piece of luck was that he was the only guest in the boardinghouse.

"It's been a slow month for us," the mother had said as she showed him to his room—and wasn't she giving him the eye even then?

Alone in the house with a beautiful mother and daughter, Bill Benedict's imagination was running away with him. He went back to his room after that first night's dinner and doused himself with toilet water, the bottle he'd gotten in Philadelphia. He was sure that one of the women was going to come to his room that night. He didn't particularly care which it was—although the young one was fresh and lovely, the older would have had more experience. Each would offer him a different kind of pleasure, but in either case it would be *some* night, he was sure.

Satisfied that he smelled good enough, he settled himself on his bed to wait, his body already responding to the excitement.

"Who goes first, Mother?" Lisa Barrows asked.

Linda Barrows regarded her daughter with great affection. She knew that, at nineteen, Lisa was still not in full bloom, and yet her daughter had already surpassed her in loveliness. Indeed, Linda thought that Lisa was even lovelier than she had been when *she* was nineteen, almost twenty-three years ago. Lisa had the slender body Linda had once had, but with larger, more rounded breasts. She had noticed the way Bill Benedict was studying Lisa's body, that was why she was going to let Lisa go first. Also, it was time for the next step in Lisa's development.

"You'll go first this time, dear."

"Really?" Lisa's face lit up with excitement, making her positively beautiful.

"Yes, dear." Linda touched Lisa's face. "It's time."

Lisa took her mother's hand in hers and kissed it.

"Oh, thank you, Mother."

"Don't thank me," Linda said, touching the index finger of her other hand to the tip of Lisa's nose, "just do a good job."

"Oh, I will, Mother," Lisa promised. "I truly will."

Benedict was starting to worry that he might have been

wrong when there was a light knock on his door. His confidence surged back. He got off the bed, smoothed his hair down with his hands while looking in the mirror, and went to answer the door.

He wasn't surprised when he saw the daughter, Lisa, standing in the hall. God, she was beautiful—and so young! His mouth started to water. He had one fleeting thought of his wife of thirteen years back in Philadelphia, but he quickly pushed it away. As a traveling salesman he met lots of willing women, and he always felt some guilt when he gave in to their charms—or they to his. It was not always easy to push away the picture of Alison that popped into his head, but this time it was remarkably easy to do.

"Lisa," he said, "I've been expecting you."

The young girl showed no surprise.

"Can I come in?" she asked.

"Of course."

She entered and he closed the door. She was wearing a simple cotton dress that clung to her every curve. He was certain that she was wearing no undergarments, and he was instantly erect.

"Um," he said, looking around the room. Why did this young woman make him nervous? "I don't have anything to offer you."

"Oh," she said, putting one hand on his chest, "I think you do, Mr. Benedict."

He could swear that his skin was burning as she touched his chest through his shirt.

"C-call me Bill."

"Am I making you nervous, Bill?" she asked, starting to unbutton his shirt.

"N-no, of course not."

"I'll bet not," she said. "I'll bet you've had lots of women."

"I've had my share," he said.

She smiled as she slid her hand inside his shirt and touched his chest. With one finger she teased a nipple until it got hard. Then she finished unbuttoning the shirt and removed it, dropping it to the floor.

"You have a very nice chest," she said, running both palms over it.

"I try to keep fit."

"You've done a good job."

Suddenly her full-lipped mouth was on his chest, and her tongue was teasing his nipples. He moaned, heard himself, and tried not to do it again. When he did, though, she laughed.

"Y-you're not a virgin, are you?" he asked.

She laughed again.

"How did you guess?" she asked. "Does it matter?"

"N-no," he said, "it doesn't."

"Let's get you out of these pants," she said and started unbuckling his belt. "If you were expecting me, you should have had them off already."

"I wasn't—I mean, I didn't—"

"You weren't completely sure I'd come?" she asked, unbuttoning his trousers.

"Well—"

"But you felt what was happening between us at dinner, didn't you?"

"Oh, yes," he said as she slid his pants to the floor, "I d-did."

"Step out of the pants, Bill."

He'd already removed his shoes, so stepping from his pants was easy.

"Mmmm," she said, running her hands up his legs to

his thighs, "you have nice legs. Just the right amount of hair."

Lisa was pleased that, although this one was a lot older than she was, he *did* keep himself in shape. He was a lot better than some of the older, fatter men who came to the boardinghouse.

She tugged his underwear down and his erection sprang into view. She tossed the garment aside, then slid her hands up his thighs and took hold of his hard penis.

She was going to enjoy this one.

Downstairs Linda Barrows waited, giving her daughter enough time to work on the salesman. The man had sealed his own fate when he started bragging that he had plenty of money to pay for the best room. At dinner, while Lisa gave him the eye, he continued to brag, and Linda decided that he would be next.

But not until they had their fill.

When Lisa Barrows took his penis into her mouth, Bill Benedict groaned aloud and didn't care. Her mouth was hot and avid, and her hands were still touching him while she sucked him.

"Jesus—" he said, reaching for her head, but she pulled away and released him from her mouth. His penis glistened with her saliva, and prodded the air, as if begging for more attention.

Abruptly, she stood up and began pulling her dress off so anxiously that she tore it.

"On the bed," she gasped, "now."

Benedict was surprised and pleased at how badly this young girl wanted it.

He got on the bed and she straddled him and engulfed him, sliding down on him hard and taking him inside.

He'd thought her mouth was hot, but this was like an inferno.

She began to ride him up and down, and he stared in awe at her perfect breasts as they bobbed in front of him. He reached for them, wanting to hold them and suck them, but she flew into a frenzy as she continued to slide up and down on his penis. She was gasping from deep in her throat, and he finally gave up and closed his eyes, moving his hips, coming up to meet her thrusts each time she came down on him. He'd never been with a woman who was so desperate for sex—and he was loving it.

When he finally exploded inside of her she screamed, and he was glad that he was the only guest in the board-inghouse.

But what was her mother going to think?

When Linda heard her daughter scream, she knew it was time for her to go up and join them. While she and her daughter were never with a man at the same time, they often watched each other, and most men enjoyed that.

She didn't think Bill Benedict would be any different. He had shown all the signs of being just like all the others.

And he would end up just like all the others.

ONE

It was to be Clint Adams's last day in Dalton, Arkansas—at least, that was what he thought. He was planning to leave the next morning, but he hadn't bargained on meeting Victoria Williams.

Actually, the day he met Victoria he woke up next to a girl named Angela, with whom he'd spent a very energetic three days. That night had been even more frantic because Angela knew it was their next to last night together. In the course of trying to wear him out she had succeeded in wearing both of them out, and she was still sleeping soundly when he was awakened by a shaft of sunlight on his face.

He moved so that the sun was no longer in his eyes and looked at Angela. She was blond, and as she lay on her stomach her hair had fanned out all around her head on the pillow. She had more hair than any woman he'd been with in recent years, not only long but thick. The

sheet was down around her knees, so that he had a clear
view of her lovely back and her firm, round butt. She was
basically thin, with small peach-sized breasts, but for a
woman as slender as she was she had a wonderfully full
ass. Just staring at it made him start to get hard.

He got on his hands and knees and straddled her, trying
not to wake her . . . yet. His penis was almost fully hard,
so he placed it on the crease between her ass cheeks and
began to rub her up and down with it. He quickly swelled
to readiness and she began to stir.

"Oooh," she said, with her face in the pillow, "what's
that?"

"I think you know what it is, Angela," he said.

"Hmm, it feels like . . . no, it couldn't be . . . is that an
oak tree?"

"Close . . ." he said.

He reached between her thighs and slid his hand un-
derneath her until he could part her with his fingers, wet-
ting her. He stroked her while she writhed beneath him,
dipped his fingers in and out of her until she was sopping
wet. As he removed his hand she lifted her butt, knowing
what was coming. He slid his penis down along the crack
in her ass until he was between her thighs. She lifted her
ass higher, giving him access, and he slid into her from
behind.

"Oooh, God," she groaned, "it *is* an oak tree."

He began to move inside of her and as he did she rose
up onto her knees and grabbed hold of the bed rail. He
put his hands on her ass, rubbing and kneading her cheeks
while he continued to drive into her. She helped by slam-
ming her butt back against him every time he moved forward, gasping each time he drove into her to the hilt. They
kept this up, increasing the tempo more and more until
Clint couldn't restrain himself anymore. He exploded in-

side of her, and she gasped and shuddered and collapsed onto her belly once again, exhausted. . . .

"I want breakfast," Clint said a little later, getting dressed.

Angela groaned into the pillow.

"Why aren't you tired like me?" she demanded. "You're older than I am."

He slapped her on the rump for that remark, making her cry out.

"Maybe being with a young girl like you invigorates me," he said. "I know it makes me hungry."

"I don't want to eat," she said. "I want to sleep more. Can I?"

"You can do whatever you want," he said. "I'm going to get some breakfast."

"Come and get me after you're finished," she said. "I have to go to work at noon."

Angela worked in a dress shop in town. They had met when Clint saw her working in the window of the shop and went inside to meet her.

"If you're still here when I get back," he said, opening the door, "naked and in my bed, I don't think you'll be getting to work on time."

"Promises, promises . . ." she said.

TWO

Clint's first breakfast in Dalton had been in the hotel dining room. It had been a mistake. The eggs were runny and the steak tough. Later, Angela had shown him a better place to have breakfast, and all his other meals. That's where he went now.

It was still fairly early as he entered the café. The waiter who had seated him the other five times he'd eaten there came over smiling. The man was always there, and Clint suspected he owned the place.

"Mr. Adams, good morning."

"Good morning, Ben."

"Eating alone this morning?"

"That's right."

"This way."

He led Clint past a half a dozen tables until he came to an empty one by the wall. It was the one Clint had chosen himself the first day.

"I'll bring a pot of coffee, sir. Your usual breakfast?"

"Yes, thanks, Ben."

The waiter walked off and Clint looked around. A couple of tables were occupied by town merchants, another by a man and a woman, probably a married couple, and still another by a man and a woman and a little boy. At a fifth table sat an extremely handsome-looking woman who appeared to be in her late forties. She was alone, halfway through with her breakfast, from which she rarely looked up. Clint got an impression of great sadness from her.

Ben returned with his pot of coffee, and at that moment the woman looked up. Briefly, their eyes met, and then she looked back down again. Clint had another impression, this one of intelligence and determination. Had this been his first day in town rather than his last—and if Angela wasn't still waiting in his bed—he might have made it a point to try to meet this woman. He found her that interesting.

Clint was into his meal when he looked up and noticed that the woman was looking at him. When she saw him look at her, she quickly looked away. Later, over his second pot of coffee he noticed her talking to the waiter, Ben. He wondered if she was that slow an eater, or if she was dallying for some other reason.

He got his answer when Ben came over to his table.

"Mr. Adams, the, uh, lady over there would like to talk to you."

"Really?" Clint asked. "Do you know who she is, Ben?"

"No, sir," the waiter said. "This is the first time I've seen her."

"Did she say what she wanted?"

"She, uh, asked me who you were."

"And you told her?"

"Uh, yes, sir. Did I, uh, do right, sir?"

"Well," Clint said, "I guess that depends on what you told her, doesn't it?"

"Uh, I just told her . . ."

"Never mind," Clint said. "Ask the lady to join me for coffee, Ben."

The waiter looked relieved.

"Yes, sir."

Ben relayed his request, and then led the lady to Clint's table. Upon closer inspection Clint guessed she was fifty or so, but still a very handsome, full-bodied woman. She had startling violet eyes and very clear, smooth skin. Women twenty years younger than her would probably kill for that skin.

"Mr. Adams?"

He stood up.

"Clint Adams, ma'am. And you are . . . ?"

"My name is Victoria Williams, Mr. Adams."

"Please, uh, Miss . . ."

"It's Mrs."

"Please sit, Mrs. Williams," Clint said. "Ben, another cup?"

"Comin' up."

Victoria Williams sat across from him and looked embarrassed.

"I'm very sorry to bother you at your morning meal, Mr. Adams—"

"Not at all," Clint said. "As you can see, I'm finished. I'm just having my second pot of coffee."

"Second pot?" she asked, surprised. "I usually have a second cup."

"Will you have one with me?"

She nodded and said, "It will be my second."

Ben brought another cup and poured some coffee for Victoria Williams. He hesitated a moment, then left when Clint gave him a look.

"Why did you want to talk to me, Mrs. Williams?"

"Well . . . will you call me Victoria?"

Clint hesitated a moment, then said, "I guess that depends on why you want to talk to me."

"I asked the waiter about you and he told me who you are."

"Just what did he tell you?"

"That you are a man with a . . . reputation."

"For what?"

"He was rather . . . vague on that, but when he told me your name—"

"My name?"

"Well . . . the name others call you by, then I knew who you were."

"You've heard of me?"

"Of course," she said, then toyed with the cup, from which she had not yet sipped. "I have a confession to make."

He waited.

"I suspected who you were," she said. "You see, I'm from the East and I've read extensively about the West."

"Uh-huh."

"I've even seen a picture of you. It was in a newspaper."

"Where are you from?"

"Boston. Have you been there?"

"Yes."

He didn't comment on whether he liked it or not, because after all this time he still wasn't sure.

"Perhaps I should come to the point," she said, pushing the coffee cup away.

As compelling a woman as she was, physically, and as much as he enjoyed sitting across from her, he was waiting for her to do just that.

"That would be nice."

"I need your help."

"To do what?"

"My husband is missing."

"You need a detective."

"I hired a detective."

"And what did he have to say?"

She hesitated a moment, then said, "He is missing, as well."

"Interesting," Clint said.

"The last time I heard from him," she went on, "was Sullivan City, Arkansas. Do you know the place?"

He thought a moment, then shook his head.

"No."

"I'm on my way there."

"Alone?"

She smiled.

"Well, I guess that's up to you."

THREE

"What do you think I can do," he asked, "that your detective couldn't?"

"Stay alive, maybe."

"You think he's dead?"

"Maybe," she said again.

"And your husband?" he asked. "Do you think he's dead, too?"

She hesitated a moment, then took a deep breath and said, "I hope not . . . but yes, I think he . . . is."

"Why?"

"If he was alive," she said, "he would have contacted me by now."

"How long has he been missing?"

"Three months."

"And the detective?"

"A month."

"Excuse me for asking, Mrs. Williams, but—"

"There could very well be another woman involved," she said, anticipating his question. "There . . . have been in the past."

"The man sounds like a fool."

"Thank you," she said, and then went on. "There have been other women, but never for very long. Even if he did have a woman here in the West, he would have kept in contact with me to keep me from worrying, or from looking for him."

"I suppose it would be embarrassing to go looking for him and find him with another woman."

She looked directly into his eyes and said, "It has been, yes."

"Forgive me, Mrs. Williams, but if your husband is as, uh, constantly unfaithful as you are indicating, why do you stay with him?"

"I love him, Mr. Adams," she said calmly. "I love him."

Clint didn't understand women.

"Call me Clint."

"Will you help me, Clint?" she asked. "Will you come with me to Sullivan City?"

He didn't answer right away.

"Do you have something important to do that would keep you from helping me?"

"Well, no—"

"Then it is simply a case of whether or not you want to."

"Mrs. Williams—"

"I can pay you," she said. "I can pay you very well."

"I'm not a detective, Victoria," he said, "but I know a few. I can recommend someone."

She shook her head.

"I was determined to do this alone, Clint," she said.

"It's just that I recognized you. This was a spur-of-the-moment thing, and I guess it was a mistake." She started to rise. "I'm sorry I took up your time."

"And wasted my coffee."

She stopped short.

"What?" She looked puzzled.

He pointed to her untouched cup.

"Oh," she said, "yes, I'm sorry. I'll pay for it—"

"Sit down, Victoria," he said, "and tell me about your husband."

She sat back down and stared at him.

"I don't know how to thank—"

"Don't thank me," Clint said. "Just tell me all about him. If I'm going to look for the man I'd like to know what he's like."

Other than the fact that he cheated on a woman like Victoria Williams . . . the fool.

FOUR

Henry Williams was a wealthy man who traveled a lot on business. That was what Victoria Williams said.

"What business is he in?"

Now she looked sheepish.

"I don't know."

"Excuse me?"

She looked at him and said it again.

"You don't know what business your husband is in?" he asked incredulously.

"My husband never discussed his business with me, Clint."

"How long have you been married?"

"Twenty-six years."

"And in all that time . . ."

"Never," she said. "It was understood that he would not discuss it with me, and I would not ask."

This baffled Clint, that two people should be married

18

that long, live together that long, and not discuss something as . . . important as that.

"Was it legal?"

"I beg your pardon?"

"The business he was in?" he asked. "Was it legal?"

She stared at him a moment, at a loss for an answer, and then said, "What an odd question."

"It never occurred to you that your husband's business might be illegal?"

"Frankly . . . no."

"How often does he travel?"

"Quite often."

"To the West?"

"About once a year to the West, but he has always stayed in touch in the past."

"Did you hear from him at all?"

"Yes," she said, "once. He sent me a telegram, said he missed me and . . . and that he loved me."

"That's all?"

"Yes."

"Where did he send the telegram from?"

"I expected to hear from him again," she said quickly.

"You don't know where it was sent from?"

"I expected to get more."

"And you didn't keep it?"

She shook her head.

"I know I'm not much help," she said, "except that I know that detective was heading for Sullivan City."

"We'll have to find out if he ever got there," Clint said. "Did you keep the telegram from him?"

"Yes," she said, "it's in my room."

"That's good," he said. "Now tell me what kind of man your husband is. . . ."

Even the way Victoria told it, from the point of view

of a woman who loved him, Henry Williams was not a nice man. He did not have any friends that she knew of, and she was sure he had many enemies.

"What kind of enemies?" he asked.

"What do you mean?"

"Politicians, businessmen, newspapermen . . . what kind?"

She thought a moment, then said, "All of those, I guess."

"Victoria," he said, "didn't you ever read anything about your husband in the papers?"

She shook her head.

"He expressly forbade it."

Clint shook his head.

"What's wrong?"

"Well . . . I don't mean any offense . . ."

"Please," she said, "speak freely. I won't be offended."

"You strike me as an intelligent woman. You're beautiful, and I would think you'd be an asset to any man's business."

She responded to what sounded like compliments with silence, because she knew there was more to come.

"Why would you live your life in the dark like that?" he asked. "Why would you allow your husband to treat you that way?"

"It isn't just me, Clint," she said. "It's the way husbands and wives live in the East. My mother lived that way, and her mother . . ."

"I guess women in the West are just more . . . headstrong," he said.

He wondered how she ever got up the nerve to come west alone to search for her husband.

"Victoria, are you prepared for what you might find?"

"I've prepared myself to find out that he's dead," she said. "What could be worse than that?"

"You'd be surprised," Clint said. "You would be surprised."

Clint knew that Victoria Williams would be—and was going to be—surprised by a lot of things she would see in her quest to find her husband, or what happened to him. He also knew that by agreeing to help her, to being her "guide," he was the one who was going to show her these things.

He was going to have to be prepared to deal with her reactions. He wondered who she was going to end up hating more, him or her husband.

FIVE

"Let me get this straight," Angela said. "You're leaving me for another woman . . . and you're telling me about it?"

"I'm not leaving you for another woman," Clint said. "I was leaving anyway, remember? All I've done now is agree to help a woman try to find out what happened to her husband."

"Hmm," Angela said, folding her arms across her chest.

When Clint got back to his room she had been dressed and waiting. When she asked him what had taken him so long, he told her.

"What's she like?"

"She's a very nice woman."

"I'll bet," Angela said, "and good-looking, too, huh?"

"Yes," Clint said, "she's very attractive."

"And young?"

Angela was all of twenty-eight.

"Oh, I guess she's about . . . fifty."

A look of relief flooded her face and she dropped her arms to her sides.

"Fifty?"

"That's right," Clint said. "Maybe older, but carrying it very well."

"Fifty," Angela said again, more to herself than to him. At least he wasn't leaving her for a *younger* woman.

"Well," she said, "the poor woman. Of course you should help the poor old thing find her husband. When will you be leaving?"

"In the morning."

"Well," she said, "that gives us tonight, doesn't it?"

"Yes," he said, "it does."

"I have to get to work," she said. "See you after?"

"Yes."

She kissed him shortly and as she was going out the door he heard her giggle and say to herself again. "Fifty."

Clint felt it was just as well Angela thought that Victoria Williams was a "poor old thing." He was looking forward to one more night with her before he left Dalton.

He left the hotel and went to the livery to check up on Duke. He was traveling without his gunsmithing rig and team, so he wasn't going to have to worry about boarding them.

He was doing less traveling with that rig these days. Also, he was doing less actual gunsmithing. He still worked on his own guns but didn't do so much work for other people, unless they were friends. He had taken on a commission to build a gun not long ago, and that had turned out badly. Not the gun, but the entire incident. Since then he hadn't done any work at all.

After he was satisfied that Duke was in shape to travel, he went to the saloon for a cold beer. The bartender there had come to know him. His name was Jed.

"Leavin' us soon?" Jed asked.

"What makes you ask that, Jed?"

Jed shrugged.

"You been here long enough," he said. "When you seen as many people as I have come and go you can tell about them. To me, you look about ready to move on."

"You're right," Clint said. "I'll be pulling out in the morning."

"See?" Jed said. "I don't miss much."

"Congratulations."

"Yeah," Jed said, "now if I could only turn it into a way to make money."

They shared a laugh and Jed went off to serve someone else.

Clint took his beer to a back table of the almost empty saloon and sat down to nurse it and think about Henry Williams. He didn't really believe Victoria when she said she knew nothing about her husband's business. That didn't matter much, though. Maybe she just didn't want to talk about it. Also, whether his business was legal or not had no bearing on whether he was missing or dead or whatever. The fact remained the woman needed help finding him, or finding out what had happened to him.

He'd never heard of Sullivan City. He wondered if it was a big enough place for a man to get lost in.

SIX

Sheriff Cantwell saw both Linda and Lisa Barrows coming toward him. Lisa was carrying a brown paper package tied with string, and Linda was carrying a box that looked like it held groceries.

"Ladies," he said as they reached him, touching the front of his hat.

"Good afternoon, Sheriff," Linda Barrows said.

Cantwell had eyes for Linda Barrows, and ideas. Oh, he had eyes for Lisa, too, but not ideas because she was too young. Well, maybe he had some daydreams, but what middle-aged—or any aged—man wouldn't about a young woman who looked the way she did. Cantwell had the feeling that when he looked at Lisa, he was also looking at Linda twenty years ago.

"Need some help with your packages?" he asked.

"No, thank you," Linda said. "We can manage, thank you."

•   •   •

Although Linda Barrows had spoken to the sheriff, they never broke stride while going past him.

"Don't turn around," she said to her daughter. "He's watching."

"I wasn't going to turn," Lisa said. "I know he's watching."

Linda smiled. Lisa was old enough now to know when men were watching and when they weren't, and she didn't react to it—except to adjust her walk when she knew they were looking.

Her daughter was coming along just fine.

Sheriff Ernie Cantwell watched the two Barrows women walk away from him and shook his head. He wondered how they made a go of it when they rarely had more than one guest at a time at that boardinghouse of theirs.

When they reached their house Lisa went to her room with her new dress, while Linda went to the kitchen. They had no guests at the moment, but that didn't concern her. The money they'd stolen from the last three or four had not yet run out, especially with what they'd gotten from that rich fellow. There were always people coming to the door looking for rooms. Of course, they turned most of them away, but when a prosperous-looking man appeared they always invited him in very warmly.

It never occurred to Linda Barrows that what she and her daughter were doing was dangerous. After all, who was there to catch on and be a threat to them? Certainly not Sheriff Cantwell. A smile from either one of them was all it took to fill his head with harmless thoughts. And they were very careful in picking their . . . clients. So far, no one had ever come looking for them . . . well, except for that detective, but together they had been able to handle him. He was, after all, just a man, and men really all wanted the same thing.

Linda and Lisa usually gave them what they wanted—actually, more than they ever dreamed they'd have—before they took care of them for good.

So she always managed to have enough food on hand, just in case someone showed up.

Lisa came downstairs with her new dress on and twirled to show it off.

"It's beautiful, sweetie," Linda said.

"Momma?"

"Yes?"

"Danny Jennings asked me to go to the dance with him Saturday."

That again, Linda thought.

"Lisa, if that's why you bought that dress I'm sorry to disappoint you."

"But, Momma—"

"I've explained to you about boys like Danny Jennings, and what they want."

"But, Momma, what about those other men—"

"That's different, honey," Linda said, cutting off her daughter. "I've told you that before."

"Momma—"

"Don't you get what you want from the other men?" Linda asked.

"Well . . . not enough, Momma."

"Don't talk like that," Linda said. "Whores don't get enough."

"I'm not a whore."

"I know that!"

"I just want to go to a dance."

"And after the dance? What will happen then, when that nasty boy tries to take your dress off?"

"Momma, Danny's not nasty—"

Linda turned and silenced her daughter with a look.

"All men are nasty, Lisa!" Linda said. "If I've taught you anything, surely I've taught you that."

"Momma, he's young—"

"The age doesn't matter," Linda said. "Fourteen, forty, or eighty-four, they are all alike."

"Was my father like that?"

"Your father was a man."

That was all she said, as if it explained everything.

"Well, then, where will I ever get to wear this dress?"

"I don't know, honey," Linda said. "Maybe after we leave here . . ."

"And when will that be?"

"When we have enough money."

"How will we ever have enough money when we always spend whatever we get?"

"Someday," Linda said, rearranging her daughter's beautiful dark hair around her shoulders, "the right man will come along, and he'll have *lots* of money . . . and we'll take it *all* away from him."

"That's when we'll leave?"

"That's when."

"And where will we go?"

"Who knows? San Francisco. New York. Maybe Paris."

"Paris, France?" Lisa asked, her eyes suddenly shining with excitement.

"Yes, honey, Paris, France."

"Oh, Momma," Lisa said, bouncing, "I'll need lots of new dresses for Paris."

"Yes, honey, you will. Now why don't you take this one off and go and do your chores, huh?"

"Yes, Momma."

"And no more talk about Danny Jennings and a dance?"

"No, Momma."

Linda kissed her daughter's cheek.

"You're a good girl, Lisa."

"Yes, Momma."

Lisa turned and went back upstairs, wondering what her mother would do after she sneaked out Saturday night to go to the dance—because that was what she was going to do!

SEVEN

By asking questions Clint found out that Sullivan City was about two days' ride west of Dalton. Victoria had come as far as Dalton by stagecoach, but to get to Sullivan City she was going to have to ride—and she assured Clint that she was an able rider.

"I ride quite a bit back in Boston," she had said. "I find it relaxing."

The morning they were to leave Clint rolled out of bed with weak legs. Angela had made sure he had a last night to remember her by.

"Already?" Angela complained.

"I have to get an early start, Angela."

Angela remained on her stomach, one eye visible, the other hidden by the pillow.

"Will you ever be back this way?"

Dressing he said, "I honestly don't know."

30

"Why are you always so damned honest?" she asked. "Can't you lie once in a while?"

He sat on the bed and put his hand on her warm back.

"Lying's a bad habit to get into," he said. "Once you start, it's hard to stop."

He leaned over, moved her long blond hair out of the way, and kissed the back of her neck. She shivered.

"Go on, get out of here, Clint Adams," she said.

"I'm checking out."

"Just tell Harlan I'll be out in a while," she said. "I just want to lie here and be sad."

"Don't be sad, Angela," he said. "It causes wrinkles."

"Get out . . ." she said playfully.

He thought he saw that one eye begin to tear up, but he might have been mistaken.

He left the room.

When he reached the livery he was surprised to find Victoria waiting for him. She saw his surprise on his face and smiled.

"I'm full of surprises," she said.

"Good," he said. "I like surprises. Do you have a horse yet?"

"I bought one yesterday, and she's all saddled."

"You are full of surprises," he said.

"Wait until you see me ride."

Clint looked around and saw three suitcases off to one side.

"Are those yours?"

"Yes."

"What do you intend to do with them?"

"Well . . . take them along, I guess."

"How?"

"Won't you get a . . . a packhorse or something?" she asked.

"Not for a two-day ride, Victoria."

One of the suitcases was a soft carpetbag.

"You can take that one," he said, "but the others have to stay—and you'll have to carry it."

"But I—"

"If you want me to go with you, you're going to have to do as I say."

She hesitated, then said, "All right."

"Take what you want from the other two and try to fit it in that one bag."

He went inside and saddled Duke, then walked him out to where Victoria was waiting with her new horse. She'd chosen well, a roan mare who looked like she could go a distance of ground.

"My God," she said when she saw Duke. "He's a monster."

"He gets the job done."

She walked around Duke.

"I hope mine can keep up with him."

"We're in no hurry," he said. "Sullivan City is an easy two days' ride from here."

Even so he took a few moments to examine her horse, lest the liveryman had taken advantage of her. Thankfully, he had not. The horse was sound enough.

"Can you ride for two days?" he asked.

"I can ride," she said. "What will we do when we get there?"

"Mount up," he said. "We can talk about that on the way."

"Don't we need supplies?" she asked as she obeyed.

Clint handed her carpetbag up to her and instructed her on how to tie it to the saddle horn. She did not look comfortable on a western saddle, but he said nothing.

"We'll only be camping one night," he said, climbing up on Duke's back. "I've got some coffee and beef jerky. That will get us there."

"Beef jerky?"

He smiled and said, "You'll see."

They rode out of town, Clint giving no thought to leaving Dalton behind. He'd left so many towns behind him over the years, and had returned to only a small portion of them. He'd only been in Dalton three days, and other than Angela it had been unremarkable.

His mind was now on Sullivan City, wondering what it would be like, and what would be waiting for them there.

EIGHT

When they camped that night they went over some things again. What Clint was doing was giving Victoria a chance to change some of her answers.

"Let me ask you something, Victoria," he said, after she had given all the same answers.

"Go ahead."

"Do you have any . . . suspicions about what your husband's business might be?"

She squirmed.

"I think he has many businesses."

"And you don't know what any of them are?"

She frowned.

"Why don't you believe me about this?"

"I told you yesterday," he said. "You seem too intelligent to let a man keep you in the dark for so long."

"Well . . . I wasn't smart in the beginning, and then as time went by it just became . . . habit."

She was still holding back, but he didn't press her. He handed her a cup of coffee and a piece of beef jerky. She stared at the jerky for a few moments before taking a tentative bite. She finally had to bite down hard and pull, and she looked as if she almost hurt her neck as the jerky gave way.

"How can you eat this?" she asked, chewing.

He snapped off a piece for himself and chewed carefully.

"It's just some nourishment," he said. "It's what you use to get by when you don't have real food."

"Well, I'll be glad when we get to Sullivan City where they do have some real food."

Clint decided that Victoria Williams would not last very long in the West, even though she was a competent horsewoman. She was just too comfortable with the trappings of the East.

"What will you do if we don't find any trace of your husband in Sullivan City?" he asked.

"I don't know," she said. "I wouldn't know where else to look."

"Would you go back home?"

"I guess I'd have to," she said. She looked at the jerky again. "I don't know if I could put up with the West for very long."

Clint had the feeling that was the first totally honest thing she'd said since they met.

By the time they rode into Sullivan City Victoria was no longer riding well. Clint got the impression that she'd never before been on a horse for more than a half an hour. He knew her butt had to be sore from the two days, but to her credit she never complained. The only thing she said when they stopped at the Sullivan City livery was that she wanted a bath.

"We'll get you a room and a bath and you can rest up," Clint said.

"What about looking for Henry?" she asked, rubbing her butt with both hands. Clint noticed—as he had on the trail—that it was a very nice butt, indeed, especially in trousers.

"We can do that after we get some rest," Clint said.

"Where will we start?"

"With the sheriff," he said. "But don't worry about that now."

Clint grabbed his saddlebags and rifle and then they walked over to the nearest hotel.

"Two rooms," he told the clerk.

The young man eyed them suspiciously as he handed Clint two keys. Clint knew what he was thinking and just smiled at him.

"Let's go upstairs," Clint said, and an exhausted Victoria simply nodded.

"One more thing," Clint said to the clerk. "The lady is going to want a bath after she rests."

"We have facilities here in the hotel," the clerk said.

"Good."

Clint and Victoria went upstairs, and Clint walked her to the first room and gave her a key.

"Get some rest."

"Come and get me in an hour," she said, hardly able to keep her eyes open. She was also limping when she walked.

"Two hours," he said, "and I'll arrange for a hot bath before I wake you."

"You're a lifesaver, Clint," she said.

"We'll see," he said as she went into her room and closed the door.

He went to his own room, dropped his saddlebags on the bed, and leaned his rifle up against the wall. A two-day ride was nothing for him and Duke, so he wasn't tired. He decided to go to see the sheriff before he woke Victoria up. Maybe he'd have something to tell her by then.

NINE

Clint found the sheriff's office after asking some directions. Sullivan City had the look of a fast-growing town. In fact, he could smell the new wood in the air from some of the newer buildings that were going up.

There was a wooden shingle on the wall next to the door of the new-looking office. It said SHERIFF ERNEST CANTWELL. He knocked and entered.

The sheriff's desk was off to the right, with a full gun rack behind it. Ahead of him was a doorway through which he could see the cells. On the left wall were some wanted posters, and just in front of the wall a potbellied stove with a coffeepot. The sheriff was standing at the stove, pouring himself a cup.

"Can I help you?" he asked. Then he said, "Shit!" with feeling as he spilled some coffee on his hand.

Sheriff Cantwell was a tall, rangy man with very big

hands which made his slender wrists look boney. He appeared to be in his forties.

"Sheriff," Clint said, "my name is Clint Adams."

Cantwell had put the coffeepot down, had switched the coffee cup to his left hand, and was shaking his right out as Clint said his name. When he heard it the man stopped short and looked at Clint.

"Adams?"

"That's right. I just rode into town."

Cantwell got a look on his face that was a cross between suspicious and apprehensive.

"What, uh, brings you to town, Mr. Adams?"

"I'm looking for a man."

"Why?"

"He's missing."

Cantwell suddenly remembered his coffee cup.

"You want some coffee?"

"Sure," Clint said.

Cantwell's hand was still wet and for a moment he looked confused.

"I can help myself," Clint said. "Why don't you go to your desk and dry your hand?"

"Uh, yeah, sure," Cantwell said, "help yourself."

Cantwell crossed the room to his desk, and Clint walked to the stove and helped himself to a cup of coffee. He tasted it and found it to his liking, black and strong.

"You make a good cup of coffee," he said to Cantwell.

"Thanks. I like it extra strong."

Cantwell was seated behind his desk now, and Clint walked to it. There was a chair across from the man and Clint took it, then tilted it so that he could see the front window and door while he was seated.

"This seems like a nice town," Clint said.

"We're gettin' there," Cantwell said. "Some new

money came to town a while back, and there are some changes bein' made."

"That new money wouldn't be someone named Sullivan, would it?"

"Yeah," Cantwell said, "how did you know?"

"Just a hunch."

"Town used to be called Melville," Cantwell said. "Town council voted to change it two years ago."

"That when they hired you?"

Cantwell gave Clint a real suspicious look then and said slowly, "Yeah, it was."

"Just another lucky guess," Clint said. "I'm probably done for the day."

Cantwell seemed to suddenly remember that he was the sheriff.

"What brings you to Sullivan City, Mr. Adams?"

Clint decided not to tell the sheriff that he'd already asked him that.

"I'm looking for a man named Henry Williams," Clint said. "He's from Boston, but was traveling in the West for a while. He seems to have dropped out of sight."

"What makes you think he was here?"

"Well, the last his wife heard he was headed this way," Clint said.

"Is she here, too?"

"She is. We thought we'd come and see for ourselves if he was here, or had been here."

"What's your interest?"

"The lady asked me to help her."

"That's it?"

"What else would there be?"

"I thought maybe . . . you know, you might have had a beef with him or something."

Clint shook his head.

"I've never even met the man. Does the name ring a bell for you, Sheriff?"

"What was it, again?"

"Henry Williams," Clint said patiently.

"Oh, yeah," Cantwell said. Clint noticed the man hadn't touched his coffee, which was getting cold on his desk. He sipped his own.

"No," the man finally said, "I don't think I ever heard the name."

"Do you keep pretty close tabs on strangers coming to town?"

"Well, yeah," Cantwell said, "after all, that's my job."

"Well," Clint said, "maybe you missed one." He leaned forward and put his empty cup on the man's desk. "I'll just have a look around town, if it's all right with you."

"Uh, sure, why not?" Cantwell said. "Asking questions can't hurt nothing, I guess."

"I guess not," Clint said. "Thanks for your help."

"Uh, Mr. Adams?" Cantwell said, as Clint reached the door.

"Yeah?"

"If you, uh, don't find him today, how much longer do you think you'll be in town?"

"Well, I'm not sure, Sheriff," he said. "I guess that will depend on his wife."

"Oh, yeah, well . . ."

"I'll let you know."

"Uh, yeah, good, let me know."

Clint left the office. The sheriff picked up his coffee cup, sipped it, and then choked. There was nothing worse than *strong* coffee that'd gone cold.

He stood up and walked back to the coffeepot, stepping

in the puddle that he'd made when he spilled some on his wrist.

"Damn."

He put the cup down, stepped away from the puddle, walked to the window, and looked out. He couldn't see Clint Adams anywhere.

What was the Gunsmith doing in his town, and what kind of trouble was he going to bring with him?

TEN

Clint took a walk around town, just to familiarize himself with the layout. It seemed like any other, with a red-light district that catered to all the vices a man—or a woman—could muster. Walking through that section he was accosted half a dozen times, usually by a woman, once by a man *hawking* women. It was early evening, and the saloons and gambling houses were going strong. Many of them had a new look to them, apparently having just gone up over the past two years since the town had changed names—and, it seemed, personalities.

It was almost two hours later when he returned to the hotel and arranged Victoria's bath.

"I'll see to it, sir," the clerk said.

"Have you ever heard the name Henry Williams?" Clint asked, on the spur of the moment.

The young clerk thought a moment, then said, "Uh, no, not that I can think of."

"What's your name?"

"Danny."

"Danny, you mind if I take a look at the register?" Clint slid a dollar across the desk to him.

"Uh, no, sir," Danny said, making the dollar disappear.

Clint turned the register around to face him and began leafing through it. He went back three months and didn't see Williams's name anywhere. Would the man have signed in under an assumed name? And if so, why?

"Okay, Danny," he said, "thanks."

"Didn't find what you were looking for?"

"No, I didn't. How many other hotels are in town?"

"A few," Danny said. "Three."

"I'll check with them, then. Thanks. Get that bath ready for the lady, okay?"

"Sure."

Clint went upstairs to wake Victoria Williams.

He had to knock several times before she finally came to the door. She had a robe wrapped around her and her hair was in a state of disarray.

"I can hardly walk," she said.

"A hot bath will help," he said.

"I won't take long."

"Take long."

"What?"

"Soak in it," he said. "Afterwards we'll get some dinner."

"When do we start looking for Henry?"

"I already started."

"What? Without me?"

"I thought I might have something to tell you when you woke up."

"And do you?"

"Not much. I talked to the sheriff, and I checked the registration book of this hotel for the past three months."

"Are there other hotels in town?"

"Yes, three."

"Then we can check them after my bath."

"Tomorrow," he said. "After your bath we're going to get some real food. Remember?"

"Food," she said, "I remember."

"Your bath will be ready by the time you get downstairs."

"What will you be doing in the meantime?"

"I'll try and find a good place for us to eat."

She eyed him suspiciously.

"You're not going to go and check those hotels while I'm in the bath?"

"No, Victoria," Clint said. "We'll do that tomorrow, together."

"All right," she said. Suddenly, she touched her hair with both hands and said, "I must look a fright," and slammed the door. When she released the robe like that it opened, revealing her underwear and some impressive cleavage. Clint managed to get just a peek before she closed the door.

"Not at all," Clint said to it.

ELEVEN

During his walk around town Clint had seen several restaurants. He decided to ask the young clerk, Danny, about them.

"The dining room here is pretty good," Danny said, "but if I was you I'd go to Ida's."

"I saw that one," Clint said, although he couldn't exactly remember where.

"Best steaks in town," Danny said, and told him where it was.

"I remember now. Thanks, Danny."

"Sure."

Clint hesitated, then gave the young man another dollar.

"Anything else I can do for you, Mr. Adams?"

"I'll let you know, Danny."

Clint found a wooden chair outside the hotel and sat in it to wait for Victoria. He watched the people walking by, some of whom greeted him even though he was a stranger. Sullivan City seemed nice enough down at this end. Later, after Victoria had turned in for the night, he'd check out the red-light district. He figured any man who was new in town would want to do the same. Maybe somebody there would remember Henry Williams.

"There you are."

He looked up and saw Victoria standing in the doorway. She looked fresh from her bath, wearing a simple summer dress. Her hair looked perfect, hanging down to her shoulders. Clint wished he had the nerve to ask her how old she was. If she was fifty, she was a damned remarkable-looking fifty.

"How do you feel?" he asked.

"Much better," she said. "A nap and a hot soak did the trick."

"I knew it would. Are you ready to eat?"

"More than ready," she said. "I'm famished. I want a huge steak."

"You're in luck," he said, "because I found out where the best steak in town is cooked."

"Lead me to it, then."

He stood up and before he realized what he was doing took her hand. She didn't pull away, so they walked along that way.

When they reached the restaurant Victoria said, "Oh, how cute."

IDA was stenciled ornately on both windows, and the inside was done in reds and greens. As they entered, a woman in her sixties greeted them at the door. Unlike Victoria, this was a woman who looked her age.

"Evenin', folks," she greeted. "I'm Ida. Thanks for eatin' with us tonight."

"We were told you had the best food in town," Clint said.

"Somebody told you right," she said. "Come with me, I've got a nice table for the two of you."

It was dinnertime and Ida was doing a brisk business, but she was able to give them a small table for two with no trouble.

"What can I get you tonight?" Ida asked. "I can tell you some of our better dishes, if you like."

"Steak," Victoria said. "I need a big steak, with all the trimmings."

Ida smiled.

"That's our specialty. Sir?"

"That'll do for me, too," Clint said. "And some coffee."

Ida looked Clint over a moment and then said, "Strong and black, right?"

"How did you know?" he asked.

"You look the type. I'll bring a pot right out. You want some cream for yours, honey?"

"I'll drink it black, thanks."

"Comin' up."

Victoria put her hands on the table and looked at Clint.

"All right," she said, "so tomorrow we start with the other hotels."

"Right."

"And then what?"

"Well, why don't we wait and see if that doesn't pan out," he said.

"We should have a plan, shouldn't we?"

"Well . . . I do, sort of."

"What is it?"

"There's a part of town I'll have to check without you."

"What part is that?"

He hesitated, then said, "Let me put it this way, Victoria. Did Henry drink?"

"Yes, but he wasn't a drunk, if that's what you mean."

"What about gambling?"

"He played cards, sometimes—oh, I see. You mean *that* part of town."

"Yes."

"Are you going to ask me if he sees prostitutes?"

"Uh, well, no, I wasn't—"

"Well, he didn't need to," she said. "If he wanted a woman . . . well, he was—*is*—a handsome man."

"I see."

Clint wondered about a woman who didn't know her husband's business. How would she know if he liked prostitutes or not? He'd still have to check the whorehouse, just to be thorough.

Ida brought the coffee and they weren't finished with their first cups when she brought their dinners out. She'd gotten everything on one large plate by piling the trimmings high on the meat.

"How's that look?" she asked.

"It looks great," Clint said, pleased.

"If you have any trouble cuttin' it you let me know and I'll make you another one."

"That's kind of you," Victoria said, "but I'm sure it will be wonderful."

After Ida left they both cut into their steaks and tasted it and had the same opinion—it was superb.

"When will you be checking, uh, *that* part of town?" she asked.

"I thought I'd take care of that tonight," he said, "after you go to bed."

"You can do it when I go to my room," she said. "I

have a Mark Twain book with me to read.''

"You enjoy Mark Twain?"

"Very much. Do you?"

"I, uh, have met him once or twice."

"Really?"

He nodded.

"The last time was in Boston, as a matter of fact."

"What was the occasion?"

Briefly he told her how a Boston publisher had wanted him to write a book about his life. As it turned out the publisher was also doing a Twain book. They both happened to be staying at the publisher's house at the same time.

"But that wasn't the first time you met him?" she asked with interest.

"No, I'd met him before that on a Mississippi riverboat."

She sighed and stared across the table at him.

"It sounds like you've had a very exciting life, Clint."

"It's interesting," he said, "that's for sure. I get to meet interesting people, like you."

"Oh, I'm not interesting."

"Victoria," he said, looking directly into her eyes, "you're a very interesting woman—perhaps even more than I think."

She got a puzzled look on her face, as if she didn't quite understand what he meant by that.

Or maybe she did.

TWELVE

After dinner Clint walked Victoria around town a bit, just to show it to her.

"Seems pretty rustic," she commented.

"That's only because of where you're from," he said. "Compared to most towns, this is pretty modern."

"Really?"

"If this town keeps growing, it could be a major factor here in the West, like Dodge City."

"Ooh," she said, "I've heard stories about Dodge City."

"And they were all true."

"Really?"

"It was a rough place."

"And this is going to be like that?" she asked.

"Maybe."

"And that's good?"

"I didn't say that," he said. "What this town will need pretty soon is a strong lawman."

"You met the sheriff today, didn't you?"

"I did."

"You don't think he's the man for the job?"

"No," Clint said without hesitation, "not from what I saw."

"Maybe it's a job you could do."

They were approaching the hotel.

"It's a job I could do," he said, "but not one I'd want to do. I wore a badge once, a long time ago, and that was enough."

They stopped in front of the hotel.

"Will you be careful tonight?" she asked.

"I'm careful every night, Victoria."

"Yes, but be extra careful tonight. Will you promise me?"

"Yes," he said, "I promise."

"Well, then," she said, "I'll see you in the morning. Good night."

"Good night."

She started for the door.

"Victoria?"

"Yes?"

The question he asked was something that had just occurred to him.

"Anyone ever call you Vicki?"

"No," she said, "never." She wrinkled her nose. "I'd hate it."

He shrugged and said, "It was just a thought. Good night."

He watched her walk into the lobby and turned away when she mounted the stairs. He headed for *that* side of town.

THIRTEEN

There were saloons, gambling houses, whorehouses, cribs, panhandlers, everything you could want from an area that catered to all vices. Clint thought that this part of town was going to force Sheriff Cantwell out of a job, sooner or later. It had to happen. The man just wasn't smart enough or strong enough to contain it. As a man came careening out of a saloon, barely missing Clint and crashing to the ground, he knew that it had already started.

There were half a dozen saloons, but he tried to imagine what kind of a place a man like Henry Williams would frequent, and he decided on the biggest. That meant a place called THE HOWLING WOLF SALOON AND DANCE HALL.

As he approached the place he heard the music, but when he entered he realized that he'd find more gambling there than dancing. There was a stage up in the front, but there was no dancing going on at the moment.

He was about to walk to the bar when a woman appeared in front of him and bumped him pretty good with her ample breasts. She was about five four, with lank dark hair and a sweaty forehead. She wasn't unattractive, though. It was just oppressively hot in the place. She even had some interesting sweat in her cleavage.

"Lookin' for a girl, friend?" she asked.

"Not tonight," he said. "Maybe another time."

"I'm Dolly," she said, and then moved off into the crowd to find an interested buyer. He didn't think she'd have a problem.

He walked to the bar and elbowed his way to it. No one seemed to mind. It was the only way to get served, and they all understood that.

"Beer," he told the bartender, who nodded and fetched it quickly. With that many men at the bar you didn't want anyone getting impatient. Nobody minded getting shoved, but they did mind having to wait for their next drink.

Clint sipped his drink, trying to keep from getting jostled. There were so many people in the place that he didn't know where to start. You didn't just start asking a crowd like this questions. If the place had been less crowded he would have asked the bartender, but at the present time the bartenders had no time for anyone who wasn't ordering a drink.

He turned to survey the room and was accosted by another girl. This one was a small-breasted, tall blonde who he also turned away. She left him with her name and the scent of her strong perfume in his nostrils. Her name was Brianne, or Diane, or something like that.

There were gaming tables all around him. Faro, poker, roulette, blackjack. He decided to walk around and look in on the action.

He came to one table and saw that they were playing

red dog. It was a fairly simple game. There were three outlines on the table for cards. The dealer placed two cards in two of the squares, leaving the center one empty. The cards were placed faceup, and you had to bet on whether or not the center card, when set down, would fall between the two end cards. The odds depended on how close together the two end cards were. Your odds were higher if the cards were a ten and a king rather than a deuce and a king.

He watched for a while as player after player tried to outguess the cards. That was why he liked poker better. You had all your cards in front of you, and even some of your opponents' cards on display. Red dog depended on one card, and you had to be lucky rather than good.

"What about you, friend?" the red dog dealer asked. "Want to try?"

"Sure, why not?" Clint said, stepping forward.

The dealer had to entice people to play, because black-jack was a more popular game, which Clint didn't understand. The best odds you could get in blackjack were two and a half to one. There were a lot better odds in red dog.

"What's the minimum bet?" Clint asked.

"A dollar."

"I'll bet five."

"Thataway," the dealer said loudly. "We got us a player."

The dealer set down the two end cards and they were an eight and a jack. There were only two cards that could fall between them. Clint decided to play this one hand and then stop, so he doubled his bet. The dealer turned over a ten, and paid Clint off.

"Thanks."

"That's it?"

"That's enough, don't you think?" Clint asked, pocketing more than twenty times what he'd bet. One play and it was a prosperous night.

"Yeah, sure," he heard the dealer mutter as he moved away from the table to make room for someone else.

He walked around the saloon nursing his beer, turning away two more offers of company. There were four poker tables going, but there were no open seats, or he might have sat down. Then again, maybe he wouldn't have. More and more Clint was starting to dislike playing poker in crowded saloons. He preferred private games now, where he also knew most of the players. Playing poker with strangers was becoming more and more undesirable. Maybe he was losing the patience it took to ride a game a few hours in order to identify each player's style. Funny, but that used to be something he enjoyed.

He moved on to the roulette table and watched the wheel go around a few times. Just while he was watching, "00" came up twice, which was amazing. What was even more amazing was that someone—the same man—had it both times. Clint watched longer still, to try to determine if the wheel was being tampered with, but he couldn't tell. Maybe the man just had incredible luck.

By the time he got back to the bar his mug was empty. He decided against having another one and simply set the empty mug on the bar.

As he left the saloon a man was leaving just ahead of him. Clint noticed that it was the man who had won at the roulette wheel with "00" twice. He was counting his money as he left, which was a foolish thing to do. You never knew when someone would take it into his head to try and relieve you of your winnings.

Even as he thought that and followed the man out, Clint couldn't realize how accurate his thoughts would be.

FOURTEEN

As Clint stepped outside he saw the man ahead of him crossing the street, still counting his money. From the shadows of an alley Clint saw three figures come into view, and he knew that his thoughts were about to be prophetic.

He started across.

The three dark figures descended on the man with raised arms, and Clint knew he had no time to reach them.

"Look out!" he shouted, but not quick enough. There was a thud as something hit the man, either on the shoulder or on the head.

Clint drew his gun. He didn't want to kill anyone, but he couldn't let the man be killed. Robbed, maybe, but not killed.

"Hold it!"

The three men turned and all went for their guns.

"Shit," Clint said, and fired.

His first shot spun one man around, but was not fatal. Probably a shoulder wound. He was about to fire again when he saw two of the men turn and run off. The wounded man looked around him and, finding himself alone, also turned and ran.

Clint hurried to the fallen man and saw his money fanned out around him. He looked around first, but if anyone had heard the shot they weren't letting it interfere with their gambling or drinking.

He bent over the fallen man and saw that he was alive. He proceeded to collect the man's money and had most of it in hand by the time the man moaned and started to move.

"Wha—what happened?" he asked.

Clint grabbed his elbow and assisted him to his feet.

"You were foolish enough to leave the saloon counting your money," Clint said.

The man looked at him, and at the money in his hand.

"And you're gonna steal it?"

"Not me, friend," Clint said. "You were attacked by three men. I scared them off. Shot one of them, in fact."

The man frowned and asked, "How do I know that?"

"Here's your money," Clint said, handing it to him, "and there's the blood on the ground."

The man took the money but did not look at the blood, which appeared black in the darkness.

"I'll take your word for it," the man said. "Thanks."

"You're welcome."

"Is it all here?"

"I don't know," Clint said. "They might have gotten away with some of it, but I wouldn't advise you to count it right—okay, go ahead."

The man seemed intent on counting it, no matter what, so Clint waited, ejecting the spent shell from his gun and replacing it with a live one in the meantime.

"It's all here," the man said, as Clint holstered his gun. "Would you do me a favor, sir?"

"What's that?"

"Would you walk me back to my hotel?" the man asked. "Those bandits might descend on me again."

"I doubt that," Clint said. "But which way are you headed?"

"Back to the better part of town," the other man said. "I've had enough for the night."

"Well, we're headed the same way," Clint said, "so I'll walk with you."

"Thank you."

"Don't you carry a gun?" Clint asked as they walked.

"Oh, no," the man said. "I don't know how to use one."

"Then you shouldn't be going into places like that," Clint said.

"Oh, I don't, not usually," the man said, "but tonight was different."

"What made it so different?"

"I was seeing double zeroes."

"What's that?" Clint asked. "What did you say?"

"I said I was seeing double zeroes."

"Explain that to me, please."

"It's fairly simple," the man said. "From time to time things pop into my head."

"Numbers?"

"Numbers, names, places," the man said. "It just happens, and when it does I act on it."

"And tonight you saw double zeroes, so you went to play roulette."

"Well," the man said sheepishly, "I really didn't *go*

looking for roulette, but I did go looking for something with double zeroes on it.''

"You didn't know that it would be roulette?"

"I don't know much about gambling. I just went in and started looking around. When I saw the double zeroes on the roulette table, I knew I had to play."

"How many times did you play the wheel before it landed on double zero?"

"Twice," the man said.

"And why did you continue to play once you hit?"

"Because I felt it would hit twice."

"And it did."

"Yes, twice in a row."

"I know, I saw," Clint said. "What I didn't see was what your bet was."

"I bet ten dollars the first time."

"And how much the second?"

"Well . . . I simply left the winnings on the table."

"Wait a minute," Clint said. "You mean you left three hundred and eighty dollars on the table for another turn of the wheel?"

"Three hundred and ninety," the man said. "You forgot my initial ten dollars."

"And they let you?"

"They laughed at me," the man said. "They felt I was going to lose."

"And you knew you were going to win?" Clint was starting to find this fascinating.

"Well, I didn't *know*, but I felt reasonably confident."

Clint realized he hadn't looked at the denominations of the bills he'd picked up and handed to the man. Now he realized they had to be thousand-dollar bills.

"At thirty-eight to one . . . you walked out of there with over fourteen thousand dollars."

"Yes," the man said, "and it's all here."

"But . . . how could you leave the initial three hundred and ninety on the table?"

"All I was risking was ten," the man explained, "my original ten."

"But why didn't you take it off and play awhile longer, making smaller bets?"

"I only meant to play until I hit once, but I just felt it was going to come around again."

"On the very next spin?"

"Yes."

"Friend," Clint said, shaking his head, "you have got some amazing luck, and an even more amazing set of balls. What's your name?"

"Chance."

"Why doesn't that surprise me?"

FIFTEEN

Chance's last name was Monroe, and he was staying at a hotel just down the street from Clint's.

"How long have you been in town, Chance?"

"Just since yesterday. And you, Mr. . . . ?"

"Adams."

". . . Mr. Adams?"

"I got here today."

"Didn't I notice you win some money at red dog?"

"You were watching?"

"I hadn't yet found the roulette wheel, and I was looking at the red dog table to see if it had double zeroes. If I remember correctly you only played one hand, and you increased your initial bet."

"Yes, I did."

"Why did you do that?"

"I had nothing to lose but ten dollars, and I decided to go for it."

"Well, I guess that's what I did, too, isn't it?"

"I guess it is," Clint said. "The stakes were a little different, though."

They reached Chance's hotel first, and in the light from the lobby Clint saw that he was a young man, perhaps as old as thirty. He was about five nine and slightly built. Clint was sure that the three men probably would have beaten him to death.

He also noticed that the back of Chance's collar was red with blood.

"Looks like you've got a head wound," Clint said.

"Huh?" Chance reached up and touched his head. His fingers came away red.

"How do you feel?" Clint asked.

"I feel fine."

"Well, it's too late to find a doctor tonight," Clint said. "Go upstairs and wash it off, and then don't go right to sleep."

"I don't intend to," he said. "I have to write."

"Write what?"

"About my experience," Chance said. "You see, that's what I do for a living. I write."

"Well, that's good, then," Clint said. "Clean the cut and then write for a while. If you feel all right after that, you'd better get some sleep."

"I will. You haven't told me your first name."

"It's Clint."

"Will you still be in town tomorrow?"

"Yes."

"Then perhaps you'll let me repay you by buying you dinner."

"I'm here with a companion."

"Bring her along," Chance said. "I'd be honored to buy you both dinner."

"All right, then," Clint said. "We'll see you tomorrow."

"Excellent. Good night, then."

"Good night."

Clint watched Chance walk into his hotel, then turned and walked to his own. He was going to take his own advice and get some rest. Suddenly he was very, very tired.

When Chance Monroe got back to his room he used the pitcher and basin on the dresser to wash off the laceration on the back of his head. He probed it with his fingers and decided that it wasn't serious. He'd been hit on the head enough times to know.

That done he pulled a bottle of whiskey out of the bottom drawer of the dresser and sat on the bed, taking an occasional pull from it. He'd really lucked into something meeting Clint, who he was sure was Clint Adams, the Gunsmith.

This case was going to turn out to be much more interesting and lucrative than he'd first thought.

SIXTEEN

When Clint woke in the morning he walked to the window and looked down at the street. Was Henry Williams out there somewhere? Today was the day to find out.

He was getting dressed when there was a knock at the door. He was surprised to find that it was Victoria, looking fresh and rested.

"We have to get started," she said.

"We have to get breakfast," he said, "and today is my day to have a bath. After that we can get started."

"I can start while you're doing that."

He reached out, grabbed her arm, and pulled her into the room, closing the door. This morning she looked great, and if she had told him she was thirty-five, he would have believed her—except that he knew how long she'd been married.

"What's wrong?"

He pointed his index finger at her and shook it while he spoke.

"Don't do anything without me, understand? You asked me to come and help you and I agreed. That means that we do things my way."

"Do you think I could be in danger asking about my husband?"

"I think you could be in danger walking around this town by yourself," he said. "This is not Boston, Victoria. Don't try to go anywhere without me, is that understood?"

"Yes, all right," she said. "I understand."

"Good. Do you want some breakfast?"

"Yes."

"Let's try the hotel dining room, then," he suggested. "How could they ruin eggs?"

The hotel dining room found a way to ruin eggs. They were runny, and Clint contented himself with biscuits and coffee—and he had to cover the biscuits with marmalade to make them edible.

After breakfast Victoria was anxious.

"Can we get started now?"

Clint decided not to keep her waiting. He'd take a bath later.

He first took her out to the desk of their own hotel and let her look through three months of the register.

"But you already looked and didn't see his name," she argued.

"Maybe you'll recognize his handwriting."

She stared at him for a moment, then said, "You mean you think he might have registered under another name?"

"It's possible."

"But why?"

"I don't know, Victoria," he said. "I'm just trying to cover all the possibilities."

"It seems silly to me ..." she said, but she looked through the book and then announced that she didn't see anything that resembled her husband's handwriting.

"In fact," she added, "I saw little that resembled handwriting. You western men don't get much opportunity to write, do you?"

"You know," he said, "I didn't notice it before, but you're a real snob, aren't you?"

She didn't take offense.

"What did you do last night?" she asked as they left the hotel.

"I won some money," he said, "and kept somebody from getting killed."

He explained everything that had happened last night as they walked to Chance Monroe's hotel.

"And you call that being careful?" she asked when he was done.

"I couldn't very well let him get killed, could I?"

"No, I suppose not."

"By the way, he wants to buy us dinner tonight."

"Us?" she asked. "You told him about me?"

"I told him I was here with someone," Clint said. "I didn't say who, and I didn't say why. He assumed that my companion was a woman."

"Well," she said, "I hope that's all he assumed."

"This is his hotel," Clint said. "We'll check here first."

"What if they won't let us look at the register?" she asked.

"We can only ask."

Asking and a dollar got them a look at it. Henry Williams's name did not appear, and Victoria did not see his handwriting.

They left that hotel and went to check out the others. It didn't take long, and only cost them a dollar at each place for the clerk, so even before lunchtime they had determined that Henry Williams had not registered at any of the Sullivan City hotels.

"Now what?" she asked glumly.

"Now we'll have to look elsewhere."

"Like where?"

"Like places I'll have to go without you."

"You mean . . . whorehouses, don't you?"

"I told you, Victoria," he said, "I'm just trying to cover all possibilities."

"Well, you can go and look, but you won't find any trace of Henry there."

"For your sake," Clint said, "I hope not."

They were walking back to their hotel.

"I guess if you did find some trace of him it would be good," she said grudgingly. "I mean, it would mean that he was alive."

"It would mean that he had been here," Clint said. "That's about all. But maybe somebody would know where he went."

"What if he never left?" she asked.

"What do you mean?"

"What if you do find him at a whorehouse, and he wants to stay there?"

"Victoria."

"What would I do then?"

"Victoria," he said, "I can see him going to a whorehouse. After all, he's a man. But why would he stay there?"

"I have no idea," she said, looking at him. "I'm just

trying to do what you've been doing, covering all the possibilities.''

They walked along in silence for a few moments, and then Clint said, ''Well, he is a businessman. What if he bought the whorehouse?''

''Oh, Lord . . .'' she said, shaking her head.

''Maybe I'll talk to the sheriff again, too,'' he said.

''Why?'' she asked. ''Do you think he might have been arrested?''

''Has he ever been arrested?''

''Of course not!''

''Well, I'll just check . . .''

When they finally reached the hotel she said, ''Are you coming in?''

''No,'' he said. ''I'd better get to it.''

''It's a dirty job,'' she said, ''but I'm sure you can handle it.''

He looked at her, surprised by the tone of her voice.

''I'm sorry,'' she said immediately. ''You're only trying to help and I'm giving you a hard time. Please let me know . . . as soon as you find out anything.''

''I will.''

She hugged herself, as if she felt a chill.

''I feel so helpless just sitting in my room.''

''Read your Mark Twain,'' Clint said. ''I'll get back as soon as I can.''

''All right.''

''If you don't want to have dinner with Chance Monroe tonight—''

''No, no, I do,'' she said. ''He sounds like a very interesting man.''

''Yes,'' Clint said, ''he sure does.''

Clint had thought about Chance Monroe a lot the night

before, after he'd turned in. In fact, thinking about the young man had kept him awake for a while.

Clint considered himself a gambler, and if he had the kind of extra sense that Chance seemed to have he knew what he'd do with it. Chance Monroe, on the other hand, did not seem to know what he had.

Clint wondered if he could get Chance to let him know the next time he flashed on a number in his mind, as he had the double zero the night before. Clint would be the first one to the roulette wheel.

SEVENTEEN

Clint went back into Sullivan City's lawless district. It occurred to him if the town continued to grow what they'd need even more than a tough sheriff would be an eastern-style police department. Then they could put policemen in uniform on the streets to control the "bad element" that frequented this side of town.

Once again Clint found himself accosted by people selling something, whether it was themselves or someone else. Even if he ever had to buy himself a whore it certainly wouldn't be a street whore. He would more likely go to a whorehouse, where they displayed their product very . . . tastefully.

Clint had no way of knowing what the sexual appetites of Victoria Williams and her husband were. Did they satisfy each other? Would he be attracted to a whorehouse when he was away from home? Or even when he was simply out of the house?

The first place he tried was not open yet, and he figured he was going to run into that problem at the other places, too. He'd actually forgotten that whorehouses didn't usually cater to late morning or early afternoon business. The girls had to sleep sometime.

He decided to start asking the street people if they'd seen a man matching Henry Williams's description. A dollar here and there had already gone a long way with hotel clerks. It would certainly work as well—if not better—with the street people of the town.

As he was approached by them to "buy" something, he instead offered them a dollar for information. Of course they were anxious to make a dollar for doing nothing, and that's just what they did. No one Clint spoke to could remember a man matching Henry's description. It didn't occur to him that they'd be lying, because they'd get the dollar anyway. Hell, if they were going to lie they'd say they *had* seen him, to try and entice more money from him.

By the time the sun reached its highest point of the day he still had no information. He thought about going to see the sheriff again, as he had told Victoria he would, but he decided against it. The man struck him as being useless, if not totally incompetent, and he'd only end up getting annoyed that such a man was wearing a badge. Instead, he decided to try some of the whorehouses again, to see if any of them had opened early.

When Chance Monroe awoke the next morning he had a headache, but there didn't seem to be any permanent damage from the night before. He sat up in bed, swung his feet to the floor, and probed the back of his head. Not too bad. Satisfied that he could function, he stood up, waiting to see if any dizziness would follow, and then washed and got himself dressed.

Today he was going to watch the women—at least until dinnertime, when he'd go back to his hotel to meet Clint Adams and his friend.

He wondered what a man like Adams was doing in Sullivan City. Just passing through? And if so, why was he traveling with a woman? Everything he'd ever heard or read about Adams indicated that he usually traveled alone. Why, then, did he have a "companion" this time?

That was something he could find out at dinner.

It occurred to him that Adams might be there for the same reason he was, but then he rejected the idea. The man was not a lawman, or a detective, or a bounty hunter, and even if he was, how would he know what was going on at the Barrows Boardinghouse?

Dressed, Monroe slipped his wrist rig on, the one that held the two-shot derringer he wore. He'd had no chance to produce it last night, and he was glad he hadn't because now Adams thought that he walked around unarmed. He liked to keep whatever edge he could get, never knowing when he would need it. He certainly didn't anticipate crossing swords with Clint Adams, but it still wouldn't hurt to keep the man ignorant of his weapons status.

He slipped on his jacket and left his room. After a satisfying breakfast he'd slip on down to the Barrows Boardinghouse and see what he could see.

EIGHTEEN

The first whorehouse Clint had stopped at earlier was now open for business. He entered and was immediately approached by an attractive young redhead in a filmy nightgown. She was not, however, as aggressive as the street girls, or even the girls he'd seen in the saloon.

"Good afternoon," she said pleasantly. He could have been entering a restaurant. In spite of the way she was dressed—displaying much of the creamy flesh of her breasts and thighs—she was not in the least flirtatious. She was very businesslike.

"My name is Amy. What can we do for you today?" she asked.

"Are you in charge, Amy?"

She was not tall, about five two, and appeared to be under thirty. He didn't think she'd be the madam, but anything was possible. In looking down at her he tried not to stare at the freckles on her cleavage. Also, the filmy gown she was wearing enabled him to see that her nipples were dark.

"You mean, am I the madam?"

"Yes."

"No, I'm not."

"May I speak with her?"

"I don't know if she's available," Amy said. "Isn't there something I could help you with?" Suddenly, her attitude became very flirtatious, and she even moved closer to him—close enough that he could feel the heat of her body.

"Wouldn't you like to come into the sitting room and say hello to the girls? I'm sure they'd be so glad to meet you."

"Actually, I don't have time for that right now," he said. "Maybe later. What I'd really like to do now is talk to the lady in charge."

"That would be Ida," Amy said. "Wait a moment and I'll see if she's . . . around."

He watched Amy's buttocks undulate as she walked away from him and wondered if this could be the same Ida from the restaurant they'd eaten in last night.

Naw, couldn't be . . . could it?

"Can I help you?"

He looked up and saw a woman approaching.

"Ida?"

The woman he'd first seen at the restaurant the night before frowned and asked, "Do I know—wait a minute. Yes, I do know you. You ate in my place last night."

"Your, uh, other place."

"And now you wish to indulge yourself here?"

"Uh, no," he said, still thrown off balance by finding her here, "I wanted to talk to you about . . . a man I'm looking for."

"We don't have men here, honey," she said. "You have to go somewhere else for that."

"Uh, no, I didn't mean . . ."

"Relax," she said, putting her hand on his arm, "I was kidding. Come into my office, where we can talk."

"Thank you."

She looked behind her, where the redhead was standing, and said, "Amy, take care of the door, huh?"

"Yes, Ida."

"Come along, Mr. . . . ?"

"Adams."

"Mr. Adams," Ida said. "Come with me."

NINETEEN

He followed her down a hallway and through a door that led to an office. The room was nothing like the restaurant or the rest of the house. If he didn't know better he would have sworn it was a man's office. The smell of leather was fierce.

He hadn't really noticed the night before, but Ida was a truly ugly woman. She had thin lips and a pugnacious jaw, and she was built large, almost like a man. He found this odd, because most madams were ex-whores who spent years plying the trade themselves; he couldn't imagine that Ida had ever been a whore.

"A glass of brandy?" she offered.

"No, thanks," he said. "It's early."

"Have a seat, then," she said, seating herself behind her desk.

Clint sat in the only other chair in the room and regarded her across the top of the large oak desk. He noticed a shadow on her upper lip that might have been the beginnings of a mustache. A strange woman, indeed.

"Do you find it odd that I'd own a restaurant and a cathouse, Mr. Adams?"

"Not odd," he said, "I was just . . . surprised."

"And now that you've overcome your surprise, what can I do for you? You said something about looking for a man?"

"Yes," he said. "A missing man."

"Who says he's missing?"

"His wife."

"Is she with you?"

"Yes."

"Maybe he isn't missing," she suggested. "Maybe he just ran away from her."

"That's a possibility."

"A very real one, in my experience," she said. "Tell me, what makes you come here to look for him?"

"I've checked all the hotels already."

"And no sign of him?"

"No."

"Have you checked the other whorehouses?"

"Not yet."

"Do you think that this man came to see one of us and liked the place so much he decided to stay?"

"I'm just trying to determine if he was ever here," Clint said. "His wife was told by a detective that he might have come here."

"Ah, a detective," she said. "Are you a detective, Mr. Adams?"

"No, I'm not."

"The wife's lover, then?"

"No."

"Then what?"

"A friend."

"You're just trying to help, is that it?"

"Yes."

Ida took a few moments to collect her thoughts before continuing.

"Was that the man's wife you dined with last night?" she asked.

"Yes."

"A lovely woman."

"Yes, she is."

"A man who walked away from her would be a fool."

"I agree."

"Is this a wealthy man we're talking about?"

"Yes."

"From the East?"

"Yes."

"So I must think back and determine if some rich man from the East came here in the past . . ."

"Three months?"

She nodded and smiled.

"Three months. My, we've had a lot of men through here in the past three months."

"His name is Henry Williams."

"Of course, that might help. I'll tell you what I can do. I'll ask my girls about him and see if anyone remembers."

"We'd appreciate that."

"Do you intend to try the other establishments today, as well?"

"I'm going to try."

"Let me offer you some assistance in that."

Clint hesitated, then asked, "Why?"

She smiled, not a pretty sight, and asked, "Why not?"

He wondered why he hadn't taken much notice of her the

night before. Maybe her ugliness was simply that much more stark in this environment.

"What's your offer?"

"I will check with my colleagues at the other houses and see what I can find out for you."

"In return for what?"

"Oh . . . that you keep eating at my restaurant while you're here."

"That's it?"

"That's all."

He stared at her.

"Don't look so untrusting," she said. "I need both of my places to make money, you know."

"Well, if that's true, then I appreciate the offer," Clint said. "It will save me some legwork."

"Amy tells me you weren't interested in my girls."

"I don't generally pay for my pleasures, Ida."

"Well, then, with me doing your legwork for you, you won't have to muster so much willpower. Besides, you have your pleasures with you, don't you."

She meant Victoria.

"It's not like that."

"Maybe not," she said, "but it will be. I saw the way she looked at you."

"You're imagining things."

Ida shook her head.

"This is my business, Mr. Adams," she said. "When someone comes into my restaurant I know how hungry they are. It's the same thing here, and I can read it in a man as well as a woman."

"She's looking for her husband."

"I'd be careful if I were you."

"Why's that?"

"If she's looking for her husband it's not because she

loves him," Ida said. "If she's told you that, then she's a liar."

Clint didn't reply.

"She has lied to you already, hasn't she?"

"I . . . think I'd better get going," Clint said. "Again, thanks for your help."

"What hotel are you staying in?"

Clint told her.

"I'll get word to you when I have something," she said. "If that man came into this part of town, I'll find out about it."

"Don't tell me, let me guess," Clint said. "You also own one of the saloons."

"How did you guess?"

Clint had to get past Amy again on the way out, and he also caught a glimpse into the sitting room. It looked as if Ida only hired the best, as she did with her cooks in her restaurant.

As he left the whorehouse Clint knew that Ida was right. Whatever reasons Victoria had for trying to find her husband, he doubted that love was one of them.

At some point, before this was all over, Victoria was going to have to tell him the truth.

TWENTY

"I don't believe it," Victoria said.

"I talked to her."

"That nice woman from the restaurant runs a whore-house?"

"I'm not making this up, Victoria."

They were in her room and he was telling her what had happened after he left her at the hotel.

"I'm . . . shocked."

"Did you notice last night how ugly she was?" he asked curiously.

"Well . . . I did notice that she wasn't an . . . attractive woman."

"What about her upper lip?"

"What about it?"

"Did you notice anything . . . well, funny about it?"

"Like what?"

He decided not to pursue the matter.

"Never mind."

"Did you see the girls who worked there?"

"Well, sure I did. One of them met me at the door."

"What was she wearing?"

"Oh, something . . . filmy, could almost see right through it."

"Really?"

"Yes."

"Was she . . . attractive?"

"Very."

"And were you . . . tempted?"

"Very."

"How did you resist?"

"Easy," he said. "I've never paid to be with a woman."

"Well, I don't wonder."

"What's that mean?"

"It means I can't imagine you ever having to pay for a woman," she said. "You're a very attractive man."

"Thank you, ma'am."

She was sitting on the bed and he was standing by the window. Now she stood up and walked over to him.

"This has been very hard on you, hasn't it?" Whether she was telling the truth or not, he felt that this was true.

"I suppose so," she said. "I'd truly prefer to be back home."

"I don't blame you," Clint said. "I guess if you weren't born here the West can seem like a harsh place."

"Were you born here?"

"Actually, no. I was born in the East, but I came here as a boy. I've been here a long time."

"Not that long. You're younger than I am."

"Not by much."

"How old do you think I am?"

He smiled at her.

"I'm not going to let you catch me in that," he said. "I don't care how old you are, you're a damned good-looking woman, Victoria."

"As good-looking as some of those young whores?"

"And a damned sight more sexy."

"How sweet you are."

She was close enough for him to reach out and grab, so he did. He pulled her to him and she came without resistance. When he kissed her she melted against him, her lips soft and pliant beneath his. She had a full, almost heavy mouth and it felt so good to kiss her that he let it go on and on, and she let it go on as long as he wanted.

When the kiss was over she stayed pressed against him, her head on his shoulder.

"Should I apologize for kissing you?" he asked.

"No," she said, "never. Besides, I kissed you back."

Suddenly, as the thought of bedding her came to him, he was aware that he still needed a bath.

"I have to take a bath and then we have to get ready for dinner with Chance Monroe," he said. "We could continue this later."

She looked up at him and said, "I'd like that. I'd like it a lot."

"Okay, then," he said, and they stared at each other for a few moments before he moved away from her. "I'll pick you up at five."

"I'll be ready."

Reluctantly, he left the room. His desire for her was suddenly very strong, and he found himself looking forward to later.

TWENTY-ONE

Chance was waiting for them in the lobby when they arrived.

"Are we late?" Clint asked.

"No," Chance said, "I just had the feeling I should wait here."

"Chance, this is Victoria Williams."

"Charmed," Chance said, kissing her hand.

"Mr. Monroe, I've heard such interesting things about you. How is your head?"

"I barely notice it anymore, Mrs. Williams."

"Please," she said, "if you're going to buy us dinner you should call me Victoria."

"It would be my pleasure."

Clint could see that Chance was charmed by Victoria, and vice versa. She was wearing a long gown with a high neck that somehow accentuated the thrust of her full breasts. Chance was wearing a dark suit and a boiled white shirt, which made Clint feel grungy, but he did not travel with such clothes in his saddlebag.

"Shall we go?" Chance asked. "I've got a place picked out, if you don't mind. It's not fancy, but I heard the food is good. It's called Ida's." After a moment he looked at them and asked, "What's so funny?"

They were greeted at the door by Ida herself. She was as ugly has she had been that afternoon at the whorehouse, and yet she seemed much more feminine here than she had there. Clint decided not to bother himself with it and just accept it.

After she showed them to their table, Chance said, "I see you two have been here before."

"Once," Clint said, "last night."

"How was the food?"

"The steak was excellent," Victoria said.

"Well, I can't very well ignore a recommendation like that from such a lovely lady, can I?"

Unlike the night before, a waiter came and took their order, and they all ordered steaks.

"So, Chance, will you tell me about these feelings you get?" Victoria asked over dinner.

"Oh, did Clint tell you about that?" Chance looked embarrassed.

"He told me you won a lot of money."

"Well . . . I just had . . ."

"A feeling," she finished.

"Yes."

"If you used these feelings for gambling more often," she asked, "couldn't you make a lot of money?"

He shrugged and said, "I guess so. I've just never thought about it."

"Can you see the future?"

"Oh, no," he said, shaking his head. "I've heard of people who claim to be able to do that. I don't believe in that."

"What makes them so different from you?" Victoria asked.

"Well, basically, they claim to be able to see the future and I don't."

"So if they would do it, and not claim it aloud, they'd be the same as you?"

Chance looked confused and amused and said, "I don't think I said that."

"Victoria, why don't you leave him alone?" Clint asked.

"I'm just interested," she complained. "I've never met anyone who could . . . who had *feelings* like Chance does."

She looked at Chance and asked, "When did these feelings first start?"

"I was . . . ten," he said, thinking back. "Yes, I think it was ten. I was supposed to go to school that morning and I had a feeling I shouldn't, so I played sick."

"And?" she asked anxiously.

Clint didn't know if Chance was telling the truth or not, but he was playing the story for all it was worth, making her wait.

"The schoolhouse burned down," he said. "Seventeen children and two teachers were killed."

"My God," she said, sitting back in her chair, "you saved your own life."

"I suppose."

"Did something happen after that?" she asked.

"Well . . . my parents figured out what I did, and it scared them."

They waited and when he didn't go on it was Clint who said, "And?"

"They put me in a home."

"Oh, no," Victoria said.

"An orphanage for boys," he said. "I really don't blame them. They were simple people, and I scared them."

"That's horrible," Victoria said. "You should hate them."

Chance smiled and said, "I don't hate anyone."

"You're an amazing young man," Victoria said. "Clint tells me you write."

"Yes, I do."

"What do you write?"

"Right now just articles for newspapers, but I hope to write a novel."

"Like Mark Twain."

"I should be so good," he said, "or so lucky."

"I think," Clint said, "that you're a little ahead of him in the luck department, don't you?"

Chance looked at Clint and said, "Maybe, although it wasn't luck that saved me last night, was it?"

"Lucky I was there," Clint said.

"Fortunate, maybe," Chance said, "but you were there for your own reasons, your own benefit, not mine."

"Well, whatever the reason," Victoria said, "it's a good thing he was there."

"I'll drink to that," Chance said, picking up a glass of water.

After dinner they went outside after bidding Ida good night. The ugly woman gave Clint a wide smile that made him feel odd.

"What are your plans for tonight, Chance?" Victoria asked.

"Oh, I thought I'd stay in my room and write."

Actually, his plans were to go and watch the Barrows Boardinghouse again tonight.

"That's funny," she said, "my plans were to stay in my room and read. Maybe some night I'll be reading a book written by you."

"I hope so."

"Let's walk back," Clint said.

"If you have something to do, Clint," Chance said, "I'd be happy to see Mrs. Williams back to the hotel."

"I have something to do, all right," Clint said, "but it's at the hotel. Thanks, anyway."

Victoria looked at Clint and blushed.

TWENTY-TWO

Without discussing it they went right to Clint's room together. When he closed the door and turned the lamp up just enough to illuminate the room she looked embarrassed.

"What is it?" he asked.

"I haven't been with anyone but Henry since we were married," she said.

"I suspected that."

"You might not like me."

"I like you very much."

"No, I mean . . ."—she motioned to herself with her hands—". . . me."

"You're beautiful."

"I'm . . . fifty-one years old."

"I don't care."

"I'm nervous."

"That's natural."

"I don't know what to do first," she said. "I feel so silly."

"I can walk you back to your room, if you like."

"No," she said immediately. "I don't feel that silly. I want to do this."

"So do I."

"All right."

"I know how you can get over your embarrassment."

"How?"

"Undress."

"In front of you?"

"Yes."

"I . . . can we turn down the light?"

"No," he said. "I want to watch you."

"Henry doesn't even watch me undress."

"Why? Because he doesn't want to, or because you don't want him to?"

"I . . . don't exactly know. All of a sudden I just started undressing before he came to bed, or in the dark . . ."

"I like to watch women dress and undress," Clint said.

"Really?"

"Really," he said. "Especially a woman as lovely as you."

"No one's talked to me like that in . . . years."

"Well, we've done enough talking," he said, unbuttoning his shirt.

"Yes . . ." she said, and reached around to undo her dress.

She had to strip off layers of undergarments but eventually it was worth it. She stood there naked and there were marks on her skin made by straps or something, but her body was full and mature and beautiful. Her breasts were firm and plump, with just the hint of sag, and he found it hard to believe that she was fifty-one years old.

"You're very beautiful, Victoria."

He knew her instinct was to cover up with her hands, but she managed to quell it and stand with her hands at her sides. Her belly was not flat, like a young girl's, but convex the way a woman's belly should be.

"Your turn."

He had begun to undress, but had stopped to watch her. Now he continued, pulling his boots off, removing his shirt and then trousers and underpants. Finally, he stood there as naked as she was. His penis was erect.

"Oh, my," she said. "You know . . . I've often wondered what a person misses from . . . from being with one person her whole life."

She moved closer to him and tentatively touched him.

"You're very . . . pretty."

"Pretty's not a word I hear a lot."

"You know what I mean."

Clint put his hands on her hips and then ran them around to touch her ass. She, in turn, put her hands between them and touched his penis, gently at first, and then more firmly.

He kissed her then, holding her tightly to him, and she kissed him back avidly. He walked her backwards to the bed and lowered her onto it. She lay on her back with her legs dangling over the edge. He got on his knees between her legs, lifted them so that they were on his shoulders. He began to kiss the insides of her plump thighs, and when he reached the tangle of dark hair between her legs he could smell her readiness.

He leaned forward and breathed on her lightly, then used his tongue to probe into hair. She literally jumped, as if struck by lightning, and gushed onto his tongue. He lapped it up avidly.

"Oh, God, what are you . . . oooh, how did you . . . Clint!"

Abruptly she reached down and pushed him away, then scooted back on the bed. She stared at him, her face flushed.

"What's wrong?" he asked. "Did I hurt you?"

She continued to stare at him in disbelief.

"What did you do?"

"That's what I asked."

"No, I mean, *how* did you do that?"

"You mean . . . touch you with my tongue?"

"Is *that* what you did?" she asked, her eyes wide. "My God, I'm fifty-one years old and I've never in my life felt anything like that. Is that *legal*?"

He laughed.

"I don't know," he said. "I never thought about it. I take it your husband has never done that to you?"

"My God, I don't think he's ever thought about doing that to me. Do you do that a lot?"

"I've done it before."

"And you like it?"

"Yes, very much. I like giving pleasure."

"And you do it very well."

"Then what's the problem?"

She brought her knees up to her chest and wrapped her arms around them.

"If you do that to me again," she said, "I think I might die."

"And if I don't do it again?"

She thought about that for a moment, then smiled and said, "I think I might die."

"Well," he said, "if you'll die if we do and die if we don't . . ."

She relaxed suddenly, released her legs and stretched them out again.

"My sentiments, exactly."

An hour later she lay in his arms, her legs still trembling.

"I've never . . . had anyone . . . do that to me," she said. "I've never felt that good during sex. My God, after that I don't think I ever enjoyed sex before." She kissed him and added, "Thank you, thank you, thank you."

"Thank you," he said, kissing her back.

"For what? I didn't do anything. You did it all."

"You let me enjoy your body."

"Oh," she said, "my body—"

"Is wonderful."

"It certainly feels wonderful," she said.

"I know."

"No, I meant—"

He laughed and said, "I know what you meant."

"We're, uh, not done, are we?" she asked.

"Do you want to be done?"

"Heavens, no."

"Then we're not."

"Good."

"We've got all night."

"Good!"

"And we can start now."

"Again, already?"

"Yes."

"I thought it took men a long time to, uh, you know, recover."

"Not this man," he said. "Not with you."

"And you don't want to roll over and go to sleep?"

"No."

She reached down between his legs to touch him and found him growing erect, already.

"You know," she said, sliding down between his legs, "the West might not be so bad after all."

TWENTY-THREE

When they woke in the morning Victoria was anxious for more. She had awakened Clint three times during the night after they made love twice. Clint was finding it increasingly hard to believe her age. She acted more like a teenage girl who had just discovered sex.

"God," she said later, "I feel like a teenager."

Clint wondered if she was starting to read minds, as well.

"I'm hungry," she said.

"That's a good sign."

"Oh, great," she said. "I'm going to start enjoying sex, which is going to make me hungry, which is going to make me fat."

"So you'll be a fat lady who enjoys sex."

She slapped his stomach.

"Come on," he said, sitting up in bed, "we'll go to Ida's."

"You think she'll have some news?"

"Maybe."

"Oh."

He turned and looked at her. She had her knees drawn up to her chest again.

"What is it?"

"Nothing."

He leaned back and tilted her head up with a finger under her chin.

"Are you having second thoughts about finding your husband now?"

"Oh, no," she said, "second thoughts are nothing new to me."

"What then?"

She bit her lip, then said, "I've been lying to you."

"That's not news."

"Okay, Mr. Smartie," she said, "I haven't exactly been lying, but I haven't been telling the truth, either."

"Do you want to tell it to me now," he asked, "or after we eat?"

She bit her lip again.

"After we eat," he decided. "Come on, get up and get dressed."

"I need a bath!" she protested. "I smell like a goat."

"You do not."

"I do to me," she said. "Would you be a dear and go down and tell them to get a bath ready?"

"All right," he said, "but then you're going to have to buy breakfast."

"Agreed."

"Done," he said.

He dressed and went to the door.

"I'll be waiting out front."

"I'll hurry."

He opened the door and she called out, "Clint."

"Yes?"

"Thank you."

"For what?"

"I think you know."

"Then I should thank you, too," he said. "Take that bath quick, huh?"

"I'll be quick," she promised.

Clint found Danny at the desk and asked that a hot bath be drawn for the lady.

"Right away, sir."

The clerk went and took care of that and then returned, looking glum.

"What's the matter, Danny?"

"My girl."

"Ah," Clint said. "Girl trouble."

"Well," Danny said, "she ain't really my girl, but I want her to be."

"What does she want?"

"It ain't what she wants," Danny said, "it's what her ma wants."

"And what's that?"

"She doesn't want her to go to the dance with me to-night."

"There's a dance tonight?"

"Yessir."

Clint thought a dance might do wonders for Victoria, who seemed on the verge of a confession that might bring her spirits down.

"Where is it?"

"Out behind the livery at the north end of town," Danny said. "It's gonna be all outside."

"So ask another girl."

"Mr. Adams," the boy said, "as far as I'm concerned there ain't no other girls in town."

"Well," Clint said, "it's been my experience, Danny, that if she feels the same way about you, she'll find a way to show up."

"Ya really think so?"

"Yep," Clint said, "I really think so. Listen, when the lady comes out from her bath tell her I'm out front, huh?"

"Sure, Mr. Adams . . . and thanks."

"Sure."

Clint went out front and found the wooden chair still there. He sat in it and waited.

TWENTY-FOUR

Linda Barrows wondered if her daughter Lisa really thought that she didn't know what the girl was planning. At her age Linda wouldn't have let her mother keep her from meeting a boy—especially if it was for a dance. All that remained was to figure out if the girl was going to use the back door or go out the window.

Linda simply could not allow Lisa to go out with young Danny Jennings. If the boy managed to get her clothes off he'd be in for the shock of his life. Thanks to her mother's education, Lisa knew more about sex than any six girls her age—but Linda didn't want anyone to know that, least of all a boy like Danny Jennings. Once Danny had Lisa—the other way around, really—there'd be no keeping the boy away from them, and the last thing Linda needed was some boy sniffing around the house, especially when they had a guest.

No, there was no way Linda could allow Lisa to go to

that dance—that is, unless Momma went with her.

Hmmm, that wasn't such a bad idea, was it? Linda Barrows hadn't danced in a long time.

A very, very long time.

TWENTY-FIVE

Ida greeted Clint and Victoria warmly, and from the look she gave him Clint was sure that she had guessed how they'd spent the night. The woman was right, she could tell when people were hungry.

"Steak and eggs," Clint ordered for both of them when a waiter approached their table.

During their breakfast Ida came over to the table to talk.

"Clint told me that you're helping us," Victoria said. "I appreciate it."

"I haven't found out anything yet," the woman said, "but there are still those I haven't spoken to." She gave Victoria a very frank look and added, "That is, if you're still interested in finding your husband."

"Well, of course I am," Victoria said. "Why wouldn't I be?"

Ida smiled at Clint and said, "Why, indeed?"

"What does she mean?" Victoria asked after she'd left.

102

"You forget what she does for a living other than running this restaurant," Clint said.

"You mean . . . she knows?"

"Just by looking at us."

"How could that be?"

"Maybe you should ask her."

"I don't think I will," she said, after a moment. "I don't think I want to know."

"Maybe," Clint offered, "like Chance, she just has a feeling."

"Maybe . . ."

They ate some more of their breakfast and Victoria said, "Clint, we have to talk. . . ."

"Uh-oh," he said.

"What?"

"I don't think we'll get a chance to talk right now. Here comes good ol' Chance, and he looks intent on joining us."

"Oh, God," she said, touching her face, "will he be able to tell, too?"

"Maybe not," Clint said. "After all, his feelings all seem to have to do with the future, not the past."

Victoria seemed relieved as Chance Monroe reached their table.

"Don't worry," the younger man said immediately, "I'm not going to join you. I just wanted to tell you how much I enjoyed dinner." He turned to Victoria and added, "It was largely due to your company, Victoria."

"You're very kind, Chance," she said, "but, please, do join us."

"No," Chance said, "I know a table for two when I see one. Enjoy your breakfast."

He left them and allowed Ida to seat him.

"See? He knows, too," Victoria said anxiously. "Is it written on my face?"

"He doesn't know."

"Then what did he mean by that 'table for two' remark?" she asked.

"Victoria," Clint said, "we're sitting at a table for two."

Victoria looked around her sheepishly and said, "Oh, yes, that's right."

"Don't look so guilty," he said. "We didn't do anything wrong."

"Adultery is not a sin in the West?"

"Well," he said, "nobody's ever been hung for it. Are you sorry about last night?"

"Of course not," she said, "but that doesn't mean I want everyone to know."

"And no one will," Clint said. "If they want to guess, let them."

"I suppose you're right."

"Now," he said, "wasn't there something you wanted to talk to me about?"

"Oh, yes," she said, looking down. "I haven't been entirely honest with you."

"That comes as a complete surprise."

"Don't make fun of me," she said. "Please let me try to explain."

"All right," he said. "I'm sorry. Go ahead. I'm listening."

TWENTY-SIX

"I'm not as ignorant about Henry's business practices as I indicated."

"I'm glad."

"Why?"

"Because you're not a foolish or stupid woman, Victoria."

"Oh, you don't know how wrong you are," she said. "I am quite stupid."

"What makes you say that?"

"I let Henry leave Boston with all of our money."

"*All* your money?"

"Well," she said, "it wasn't . . . you see, we were not quite as . . . well-off as I indicated."

"You were at one time, though, weren't you?"

"Oh, yes," she said, "but that was before Henry lost most of it. You see, you were right about his being involved in illegal activities."

Clint just nodded.

"And I knew about it. I tried to get him to change his business, but he refused. That's when he was doing quite well . . . and then things started to go bad."

"And he ran?"

She nodded.

"And took whatever money we had left. I had just enough to hire a detective, and then make this trip." She looked away from him and added, "I'm almost broke. I—I don't know how I'm going to pay you."

"I never said I wanted to be paid," he reminded her. "Don't worry about that."

"So you see, I don't really feel guilty—well, I *shouldn't* feel guilty—about last night, because I'm no longer in love with my husband. To be quite frank, I wouldn't be that disappointed if he were dead, except I'd like to know where the money went."

Clint digested what she'd told him.

"Do you hate me?" she asked.

"Of course not—uh, can you pay for breakfast?"

She stuck her tongue out at him.

"Yes, I can pay for breakfast."

"Then I don't hate you in the least."

"No, really . . . are you disappointed in me?"

"No," he said, "as I told you, I'm glad you're not the ignorant woman you pretended to be. The better I got to know you, *that* would have disappointed me, if it were true."

"Then you'll continue to help me find him?"

"We'll keep on looking," he said, but he didn't say what would happen if it turned out he wasn't here in Sullivan City.

But she wouldn't let it go at that.

"What if he's not here?" she asked.

"Well . . . we should deal with that if and when we come to it."

"No, I'd like to talk about it now," she said. "I don't know what I'd do if he's not here. I don't expect you to drag me all around the West looking for him."

"I have some friends who might be able to help you," he said.

"Friends?"

"I know some detectives. There's a man named Talbot Roper in Denver; he's the best private detective I know."

"Is he expensive?"

"Yes," Clint said, "but you could work something out where you'd pay him when he finds your husband and you get your share of the money."

"If he hasn't spent it all by then."

"Is he a spendthrift?"

"Actually, no," she said. "He didn't spend the bulk of it, he lost it in illegal deals. He can actually make money stretch quite far."

"Well, if that's the case then there'll be something left when you catch up to him."

"Sometimes," she said, "I think I could kill him myself."

"Well, I won't be able to help you with that."

"Oh," she said, looking down at her food, "I could never actually do it."

"Come on," he said, "eat up and we'll get started again, today."

"Doing what?"

"Looking," Clint said. "Also, I can send Roper a telegram asking him if he'd be available to help you from here on in."

"So you could get back to your life."

"Yes."

She nodded.

"I understand. It was presumptuous of me to ask your help in the first place."

"I'm glad you did," Clint said. "It gave us a chance to spend some time together."

"We still have a few days, at least."

"Yes."

"We could probably save money on one of the hotel rooms—I mean, if you're interested in, uh—"

"That sounds like a good idea to me, Victoria."

She smiled and said ruefully, "Maybe the first one I've had in some time."

"I'm sure you'll be able to come up with a few more along the way."

They finished their breakfast and spoke with Ida one more time before leaving.

"I'll try and have something for you by the end of the day," she said. Then she looked at Clint slyly and said, "Maybe you can come by my other place later tonight."

"I'll see you later," he said, nodding.

Outside Victoria said, "She wants you to come by the whorehouse?"

"I guess that's what she meant."

"I think I should go with you, this time."

"Don't you trust me?"

"Oh," she said, "I trust *you*. . . ."

On the way back to the hotel Clint told Victoria about the dance Danny Jennings had told him about.

"Tonight."

"Yes," he said. "Do you like to dance?"

"I love to dance."

"Good," he said, "then we can go. You need a little time to relax."

"What about last night?"

He gave her a look and said, "I don't think what we did last night qualifies as relaxing."

"No, I guess not," she said. "My legs are *still* weak."

"Not too weak to dance, I hope."

"No," she said, "if you can dance, so can I."

"Good."

"Oh, my . . ."

"What?"

"I have nothing to wear to a dance," she said. "I wonder if there's a dress shop in town."

TWENTY-SEVEN

Chance Monroe still felt groggy even after breakfast and coffee. He'd been out late watching the Barrows' house each of the past three nights and he was starting to feel the effects. Nothing was breaking on its own, so he decided that it might be time to push things. If he wanted to do that, though, he was going to need help.

And he thought he knew just the man to ask.

Clint wasn't quite sure what to do with the rest of the day, since they were really just waiting on Ida to supply information. He thought it was a good thing, then, to let Victoria go dress hunting for the dance. While she did that he went to the telegraph office to send a telegram to Talbot Roper, as he had promised Victoria. That done he decided to wait at the hotel for the reply.

As he approached the hotel he saw a stunning young woman with long dark hair come out and start up the street. She looked about nineteen or twenty years old.

As he entered, Danny was behind the front desk, and he was positively beaming from ear to ear.

"Well, you look happy."

"Did you see her?" he asked. "She just left."

"I saw her," Clint said. "She's a beautiful girl."

"That was Lisa, Lisa Barrows."

"Did she come to talk about the dance?"

Danny nodded.

"She said she'd sneak out and meet me there. It was just like you said, Mr. Adams."

Clint had not gotten a real good look at the girl, but he had the impression that she was probably older than her years. He wondered if Danny Jennings would be able to handle such a girl.

"I hope it works out, Danny."

"It will," Danny said, "I know it will."

"Well, we'll see you at the dance," Clint said.

Danny nodded enthusiastically. As Clint turned to go upstairs he saw Chance Monroe enter the lobby.

"Looking for me, Chance?"

"As a matter of fact, I was," the younger man said. "Can we go someplace and talk?"

"We can go into the hotel dining room, have some coffee."

"That sounds fine."

They went into the dining room, got a table, and ordered a pot of coffee.

"What's on your mind?" Clint asked.

"I have a confession to make."

"About what?"

"About what I do for a living."

"Okay," Clint said, "I'll bite. What do you do for a living?"

"I'm a detective."

"You're kidding."

Chance looked stung.

"Why do you say that?"

"Don't take offense," Clint said. "It's just that I just came from the telegraph office. I sent a telegram to a detective friend of mine."

"Who was that?"

"Talbot Roper."

Chance's mouth dropped open.

"You know Talbot Roper?"

"I do," Clint said. "For a long time."

"My God," Chance said, "he's the best in the business."

"Yes, he is."

"I'd give my left arm to work with him," Chance said. "I could learn a lot."

"When did you start in the business?" Clint asked.

"To tell you the truth," Chance said, "this is my first case."

"What did you do before this?"

"Not much of anything, actually," Chance admitted. "I drifted around and tried to make a living the best I could."

"What about using this extra *sense* of yours, these feelings that you get."

"I have a confession about that, too."

"You don't have that ability?"

"No, I do," he said. "What I told you about my childhood was true. No, my confession is that my *ability*, as you call it, is more trouble than it's worth—at least, it has been up to now."

"What about the other night, at the roulette wheel?"

Chance brightened some at the reminder of his big score.

"That was actually the first time I'd ever used it for gambling. That money is going to help me a lot."

"Maybe you could keep on using it for gambling."

"I'm really not much of a gambler," he said. "I'd thought that if I became a detective I might finally be able to put this ability to good use."

"Well, then," Clint said, "what was it you wanted to see me about?"

"I need help on this case I'm working on," he said. "Working alone is starting to wear me out."

Clint did notice that the younger man had bags beneath his eyes.

"Why don't you tell me what the case is," Clint said, "and we can talk about it."

TWENTY-EIGHT

"I think these two women in town are killing men."

"What?"

Chance nodded.

"That's not the oddest part," he said. "They're mother and daughter."

"What makes you think they're killing people?"

"Not just people," Chance said. "Men."

"Okay," Clint said, "what makes you think they're killing men?"

"I get a very bad feeling when I'm near their house."

Clint waited for more, and when it didn't come he said, "Is that it?"

"Well, no . . ."

"What brought you here in the first place, Chance?" Clint asked.

"My sister."

"Your sister. What's she got to do with this?"

"She asked me to come and look for her husband."

"Her husband is missing?"

He nodded.

"You see," Chance said, "if I can do this, then I'm on my way to being a private detective."

"I'm missing something here," Clint said. "Tell it to me from the beginning."

"It's really simple."

"Then *tell* it simple," Clint said, "from the beginning."

"My brother-in-law is a traveling salesman named William Benedict—we call him Bill."

"Where are you from?"

"Philadelphia," Chance said. "That's where we live—me, my sister, and Bill."

"All right," Clint said, "I'm with you so far."

"Bill travels through the West to make his living. He's away sometimes months at a time, but he stays in touch with my sister, Alison."

The story sounded familiar, only when Victoria told it, it had been a lie.

"The last time she heard from him he said he was heading for this town. His telegram said it was a growing community, and he thought he could make a killing. That was the last she heard of him."

"So she asked you for help."

"Well, not exactly."

"What, then?"

"She wanted to hire a detective."

"And you didn't let her."

"Why spend the money?" he asked. "I thought I could find him myself, so I came here."

"And have you found any sign of him?"

"No."

"And what about these women?"

"They run a boardinghouse here in town. I had checked with all the hotels, looking for Bill, and somebody suggested that he might have gone to the Barrows Boardinghouse."

A boardinghouse. Why hadn't Clint thought of that?

"Wait a minute," Clint said. "Did you say Barrows?"

"That's right," Chance said. "The place is run by Linda Barrows and her daughter—"

"Lisa."

"Then you know about them?"

"No," Clint said, "I just saw the daughter today, for the first time."

"Isn't she beautiful?" Chance said. "And so is the mother."

"What makes you think they're killing men?"

"I went there to ask about Bill," Chance said. "Even before they opened the front door I got a bad feeling about the place. A *cold* feeling. I've only had that feeling once before in my life."

"When?"

"When a friend of mine died."

"So?"

"He was a hundred miles away," Chance said, "and I knew the exact moment he died, because I got that same cold feeling."

"And this was the feeling you had at the Barrows' house?"

"Yes," he said. "When I asked them about Bill they said they'd never heard of him."

"They could have been telling the truth."

"I don't think so."

"Even if they weren't," Clint said, "it's a big leap in

logic to assume that they not only killed him, but have killed others.''

"The man you're looking for," Chance said, "Victoria's husband.''

"What about him?''

"Have you checked the boardinghouse?''

"No," Clint said, "I didn't even know about the boardinghouse.''

"I think you should check it," Chance said. "In fact, I have an idea.''

"What kind of an idea?''

"An idea where we can work together to find out just what's going on in that house.''

"I'm not here to find out about that house.''

"I know," Chance said, "you're here to find Henry Williams. I suggest we both work together and maybe we'll each get what we want.''

"Do you have a plan?''

"I do.''

"And what is it?''

"I think you should check into the boardinghouse.''

"That's your plan?''

Chance nodded.

"I should check into a boardinghouse which is run by two women, and you're sure that these two women are killing men.''

"Right.''

Clint shook his head and said, "Sounds like a hell of a plan.''

"I know.''

Clint got to his feet and said, "Good luck finding someone who likes it.''

TWENTY-NINE

"Wait, wait, wait," Chance said, "don't be so hasty. Come on, sit back down."

Reluctantly, Clint did so.

"Why don't *you* go and check in?" Clint asked.

"I can't," Chance said. "They've seen me already. They'd never believe me as a man with money looking for a place to stay."

"As a man with money?"

"Look," Chance said, "let me explain about my brother-in-law. I knew things about him that my sister didn't—or that she didn't want to."

"Like what?"

"He liked to chase women," Chance said. "He liked to chase them and catch them."

"So your brother-in-law cheated on your sister."

"Every chance he got."

"What else?"

"He liked to brag."

"About what?"

"About everything," Chance said, "but especially about—"

"Sex?"

Chance shook his head.

"Money. I'll say one thing for the son of a bitch, he was a damned good salesman."

"And that meant he always had money on him."

"Right."

"Let me fill in the blanks here," Clint said. "Your brother-in-law—Bill Benedict?—comes to this boarding-house run by two beautiful women and immediately begins to flash his money to impress them."

"Right."

"And you think they killed him for it?"

"Right."

"And did what with the body?"

Chance shrugged.

"Buried it someplace, maybe."

"Two women?"

"You never heard of women killing somebody?"

"Oh, I've heard of it."

"So why not? What if that's what they do in that board-inghouse? They wait for men with money to come along and they kill them for it."

Clint thought about it.

"That could be what happened to your guy, Williams."

"Maybe."

"I did some checking," Chance said. "Listen to this. There is rarely more than one person staying at the Bar-rows' house at a time . . . and it's usually a man."

"Have you talked to the local sheriff about this?"

"Have *you* talked to the local sheriff?"

"I see what you mean," Clint said.

"He gets stars in his eyes whenever anybody mentions either Linda or Lisa Barrows."

"He's not very smart to begin with."

"That's an understatement."

"Just let me think about this for a minute."

"What is there to think about?" Chance asked. "I've been watching that house for three days and nights, and no one has gone in or out except those two women. Somebody needs to get inside, Clint."

"There's a dance in town tonight."

Chance sat back.

"A dance? What's that got to do with anything?"

"The clerk at my hotel says that Lisa Barrows is going to sneak out of the house to meet him at the dance."

"So?"

"What if the mother went to the dance, as well?"

"Is she going to the dance?"

"I don't know," Clint said, "but if she does, that would leave the house empty, wouldn't it?"

"Hey, that's right," Chance said. "Are you going to the dance?"

"I am," Clint said, "that is, Victoria and I are."

"So if both women are there you could slip away—"

"*You* could slip away and check out the house," Clint corrected him. "Remember, you're the detective."

THIRTY

"Lisa?"

"Yes, Momma?"

"You don't have to sneak out tonight."

Lisa looked at her mother across the table. They were having lunch.

"What?"

"You heard me."

Lisa played with her food.

"I wasn't, Momma."

"Yes, you were."

Lisa looked at her mother.

"How did you know?"

Linda laughed.

"Because that's what I would have done at your age."

"Really?"

"Really."

"Then I can go?"

"We can go."

"What?"

"I'm going with you."

Now Lisa gaped at her mother.

"You're gonna dance?"

"Sure," Linda said, "if someone asks me. Why, you don't think your mother can dance?"

"I . . . guess I never thought about it."

"Maybe I'll dance with Danny Jennings."

"Oh, Momma . . . he's too young for you."

"Too young to dance with?"

"Yes," Lisa said. "Besides, he'll be dancing with me."

"And that's all he'll be doing with you."

"Oh, Momma . . ."

"Finish your lunch, Lisa."

"What are you going to wear?"

"A dress."

"Do you have a dress?"

"I have lots of dresses."

It occurred to Linda that Lisa only saw her in Levi's or naked, when they had a male guest.

"Momma?"

"Yes?"

"We haven't had a guest in a while."

"I know."

"Do we need money?"

"No," Linda said. "That last fella actually did have lots of it, not like some of the other liars."

"Then we don't need another guest?"

"We don't *need* one," Linda said, and then added, "not for money, anyway."

"Why do we have to do it that way, Momma?"

Linda knew what her daughter was talking about, and

they had discussed it many times before. Linda had drummed it into Lisa's head as a child, and also since Lisa was sixteen—the first time she'd been with a "guest."

"It's what men deserve, Lisa," Linda said. "They're all liars and cheats."

"All of them?"

"Yes."

"Even Danny?"

"If he's not now," Linda said, "he soon will be."

"I don't see the harm—"

"Lisa!"

"Yes?"

"Finish your lunch," Linda said. "When you're done I'll take you upstairs and show you my closet. You'll see that I have dresses."

"You need a new dress, like I have."

"No," Linda said, getting up and carrying her dish to the sink, "I don't."

"If you want a man to dance with you—"

Linda's laughter cut Lisa off.

"Lisa, it's never hard to get a man to dance with you," Linda said. "And when they're dancing, and their arms are around you, they're only thinking about one thing."

"What's that, Momma?"

Sometimes Linda wished that Lisa was half as smart as she was beautiful.

She pointed to the food still left on her daughter's plate and said, "Eat."

THIRTY-ONE

"What do you think?"

Victoria twirled so Clint could look at her new dress. Her enthusiasm probably should have been out of place on a woman her age, but it wasn't.

"It's not too daring, is it?"

It was blue, and shimmery, and while the neck scooped enough to show some cleavage, he didn't think it was too daring, and said so. In fact, if a saloon girl had been wearing it, it would have been too sedate. For a town dance, it was probably just right.

"It's perfect."

"Is something wrong?"

"We have to talk," he said.

They had given up her hotel room and she had moved into his.

"Let me take this off and then we can talk."

She removed the dress in front of him, having come a

long way in such a short time since her shyness the night before. Sex went a long way toward bringing a man and a woman together. Unfortunately, sometimes it also worked the other way around.

He waited while she put the dress away and then donned something new and less festive. That done she came over and sat on the bed next to him.

"What is it?"

He told her everything that Chance Monroe had told him and she listened without interrupting.

"Do you believe him?" she asked when he was finished.

"I don't even know if he believes him," Clint said.

"What are you going to do?"

"Well . . ." Clint said, and went on to explain about the dance.

"What if the mother doesn't come?"

"I have a feeling she will."

"Why?" Victoria asked. "Are you starting to get feelings the way Chance does?"

"No," he said, "I'm basing my guess on logic."

"What's your logic?"

"I saw the daughter today."

"Really? Where?"

"Here downstairs," Clint said. "She's the girl Danny wants to take to the dance."

"You told me about that," she said. "You told him that if she wanted to go with him she'd find a way."

"Right. She told him today that she'd sneak out and meet him there."

She shook her head, puzzled, and asked, "Where's your logic?"

"Here it is," Clint said. "Do you think there has ever

been a daughter who thought of doing something that her
mother hadn't thought about doing first?''

"No," she said. "My mother always told me that I
couldn't fool her because anything I did she had already
done when she was my age.''

"Right. So don't you think that this girl's mother
knows she's going to try to sneak out and go to the
dance?''

"So, she'll be there to stop her.''

"Or?''

Victoria hesitated a moment, then said, "Or she'll go
with her.''

"Right," Clint said, "as a chaperone.''

"And that's when one of you will go to the house and
take a look.''

"Not one of us," Clint said, "Chance.''

"Right," she said. "You'll have to dance with the
mother to keep her busy.''

"I will?'' He hadn't thought of that.

"Of course you will," she said. "You can't take a
chance that she'll go back to the house and catch him.''

"And you won't mind?''

"Of course not," she said. "You don't think I'll be
standing there watching you, do you? There'll be plenty
of other men to dance with.''

"I'm sure there will be.''

She leaned against him and he could smell her hair.

"Will you be jealous when I'm dancing with someone
else?''

"No.''

"Why not?''

"Because when the dance is over you'll be coming
back here with me," he said, "and when we leave the
dance together, other men will be envious of me.''

"Oooh," she said, "you really know the right things to say to a woman, don't you?"

"Do I?"

"You know you do," she said, "but then I'll bet you've had lots of practice."

"I—"

"Never mind," she said. "The remark doesn't call for an answer."

"What do you think of the suggestion that Henry might have been involved with these women?" Clint asked.

She shrugged and said, "Involved how? He might have taken a room and been killed? I suppose it's possible. What if we just went over and asked if he'd ever stayed there?"

"I don't want them to see me—"

"What if I did it?"

"I don't think—"

"Wait," she said, warming to the idea, "don't you see? I can go over and ask, and if they say no and we find out they lied we'll be able to go to the law."

"Not just with that."

"No, but it would help to know if they'd lie about it."

"And if they say yes?" he asked. "If they say, sure, he stayed here one night and then left? Then what?"

"I don't know," she said. "I'm not the detective."

"Neither am I. Chance is."

"This is his first case," she said. "It's too bad we don't have someone here who's more experienced, like your friend."

"Speaking of whom . . ." he said, putting his hand in his pocket.

Talbot Roper's reply had come while he was out, and Danny had handed it to him when he returned. He'd read it and stuffed it into his pocket.

He handed it to Victoria now and let her read it.

"This is wonderful," she said, handing it back.

"Keep it."

The telegram said that Roper would be very willing to help Victoria Williams find her husband if they failed to locate him in Sullivan City. He further said that she wouldn't have to come to Denver. He would meet her wherever she said.

"He only agreed because you're friends," she said.

"What's wrong with that?" he asked. "Why shouldn't one of my friends help another?"

"I'm so glad I ran into you in Dalton," she said.

"Me, too."

She slid her hand into his lap and added, "For more reasons than one."

"Aren't you ever satisfied, woman?"

"No," she said, undoing his belt, "never."

THIRTY-TWO

The area behind the livery stable was rigged with fancy lanterns and streamers and balloons and other decorations. There were booths littered about selling cakes and spices and candies and food. Clint didn't know if this was a special occasion, or if it was simply a weekly or monthly event. It looked as if most of the town had turned out for it.

On a raised stage was a small group of musicians with guitars and violins, and people had already begun to dance.

"How festive," Victoria said.

"It sure is."

"Do you see them?"

"See who?"

"The two women?"

"I've never seen the mother, so I don't know what she looks like," Clint said, "but I don't see the daughter anywhere. There's Danny, though. Let's go and talk to him.''

Danny Jennings was standing off to the side, looking uncomfortable in a jacket and tie and tapping his foot to the music—or trying to. He was woefully out of time with it.

"Hello, Danny."

"Oh, hello, Mr. Adams, ma'am."

"Where's your girl?"

Glumly, Danny said, "I don't see her, sir. Maybe her mama caught her."

"She'll be here," Clint said, "don't worry."

"I hope so."

Clint saw Chance Monroe arrive.

"Point her out when she gets here, will you? Mrs. Williams would like to see her."

"Yes, sir."

To Victoria he whispered, "Stay with him," and he went to meet Chance.

"What are you doing here?" Clint asked. "I thought you were going to watch the house."

"What's the difference?" Chance asked. "When they get here and I'm sure they'll be here for a while I'll go over there."

"When they get here," Clint said, "I'll ask the mother to dance. Danny will take care of the daughter for us."

"That's good thinking," Chance said. "With you dancing with her I won't have to worry about being caught."

"Now all we need is for them to get here."

"Yeah."

"Well, dance with somebody."

"What?"

"You don't want to attract attention," Clint said. "Dance with somebody."

"I, uh, don't dance well."

"Some nice girl will teach you," Clint said. "All you have to do is ask."

Chance frowned, but went off to find a likely victim. Clint turned and saw Victoria waving at him frantically.

"What—" he asked when he reached her, but she cut him off.

"Look!"

Clint looked in the direction she indicated and saw two women standing together. One was the young girl he'd seen earlier. The other was obviously her mother, a full-bodied, dark-haired, earthy, sensual-looking woman in a simple dress.

"Wow!" Victoria said.

"They do make a pair, don't they?" Clint asked.

"They're lovely."

"Danny," Clint said, "there's your girl."

The boy swallowed hard and looked at Clint.

"She's with her ma."

"So?"

"I . . . can't go over there while she's with her ma."

Clint looked around and saw that Chance was still not dancing with anyone.

"Victoria," he said, "go and dance with Chance, will you? He looks lost."

She looked at him and he jerked his head, indicating that she should leave.

"All right."

As she went off to grab Chance and take him on the dance floor, Clint said, "Danny, I'm going to do you a big favor. . . ."

THIRTY-THREE

"Momma, look," Lisa said.

"I see him," Linda said.

Both women saw the man approaching them, a man the mother's age, not the daughter's. An attractive, self-assured man.

"Would you like to dance?" he asked Linda, when he reached them.

Linda gave her daughter a smile and said to the man, "Yes, thank you."

He extended his arm and she took it and allowed him to lead her out onto the dance floor.

Danny Jennings watched as Clint Adams took Linda Barrows onto the dance floor. From across the way Lisa Barrows's eyes met his. He smiled and started for her, and she met him halfway.

"You came," he said.

"I told you I would."

"Would you like to dance?"

She looked around them and then said to him, "I didn't come here to dance."

She knew her mother would be angry, but she had an itch that had to be scratched, and she knew she could use Danny Jennings to scratch it.

"Uh . . ." Danny said, swallowing hard.

"Come on," Lisa said, taking his hand and leading him *away* from the dance floor.

Chance Monroe was dancing—badly—with Victoria when Clint started to dance with Linda.

"She's attractive, isn't she?" Victoria asked.

"Personally," Chance said, "I prefer the daughter. She's younger." He suddenly remembered who he was dancing with and said, "Uh, I mean—"

"I know what you mean, Chance," Victoria said. "Don't you think you better get going?"

"Uh, yeah, I should," he said. "Thanks for the dance."

"Thank you."

He left her standing there and walked off, but there was another man there in seconds to take his place.

"Would you like to dance?" he asked.

"Why, yes," she said, "I'd love to."

"What's your name?" Linda Barrows asked.

"Clint."

"Just Clint?"

"That's all we need for now," he said. "After all, we're just dancing."

A smooth talker. She'd met a lot of smooth talkers in her time, but at least this one could dance.

"I haven't danced in a long time," she said.

"That's a shame," he said, "but to tell you the truth, neither have I."

"You're doing real good," she said.

"So are you."

"Are you just passing through town?"

"Yes," he said. "I'm, uh, looking for a place to stay." He didn't know why he was saying that, but the words came out before he could stop them.

"There are a lot of hotels in town."

He smiled and said, "I prefer something with a little more . . . privacy."

"Could it be you're looking for something cheaper?" she asked.

"Oh, no," he said, "money is not a problem."

"Really?"

"I've got plenty of money."

"Well, then," Linda Barrows said, "maybe we can help each other."

When Chance Monroe reached the Barrows Boarding-house it was dark. The women had not left a light burning inside. The moon was bright enough for him to see outside, but he didn't know what he'd do once he was inside. He certainly wouldn't be able to light a lantern. He decided he'd just have to wait for his vision to adjust to the darkness inside before he could move around, but even before he could worry about that he had to get inside.

He decided against trying the front door and instead went around to the back of the house.

Lisa Barrows led Danny Jennings into the livery stable, which was abandoned because of the party going on out back.

"No one will come in here," she said.

"But . . . what if they do?" Danny asked nervously.

"Danny," she said, turning to face him, "don't you want me?"

He swallowed hard and said, "Uh, sure I do, but . . . it's dark in here."

"Trust me," she said in his ear, "we won't need to see."

Her breath on his ear was the last straw. He felt as if he was going to burst from his pants.

"Come on," he said, grabbing her hand this time, "let's go up in the hayloft."

THIRTY-FOUR

While dancing with other men Victoria Williams had to admit that Clint and Linda Barrows made a handsome couple. She was, after all, more his age. Clint seemed very intent on dancing with her, and they were keeping up a running conversation.

She wondered what they were talking about.

"A boardinghouse?" Clint asked. "Really?"

"Yes, really," Linda said. "Why would I lie?"

"Oh, I'm sorry," Clint said, "I didn't mean to imply . . . I just thought . . . you don't look like a landlady."

Linda laughed and said, "Well, I am."

She felt good in his arms, solid and warm, and she smelled good. She kept her hips pressed to his, so that he was sure she could feel his erection through his pants. He found it hard to believe that she was a man-killer—if Chance Monroe was right about her.

"Would you like to take a look at it?" she asked.

"Sure," he said. "When?"

"We could go there now."

"Oh," he said, thinking quickly, "I don't think I want to go just yet."

"Why not?"

He pulled her more tightly to him and said, "We're just starting to move well together."

"You know," she said, "you don't look like a man with money."

"Oh? What does a man with money look like?"

"Well," she said, "he usually dresses so that people know he has money."

"Uh-huh, really?"

"And he acts like he has money," she went on. "Rich men usually want people to know they're rich."

"Well," Clint said, "I never said I was rich. I just said money wasn't a problem."

"Well, you're still the only man I ever met that didn't brag about it."

"I don't have to brag about it."

"Why not?"

"Because I'm a good dancer."

Linda laughed, and again he tried to picture her killing somebody, and it came hard.

Danny was hard, and when Lisa opened his pants and pulled them down his erection sprang into view. It was dark inside the stable, but Lisa's eyes had adjusted to the darkness and she could see that he had a smooth, pretty penis.

"Oh," she said, and touched him lovingly with both hands.

It was all Danny Jennings could do not to explode right

there and then. He was so excited that he was afraid he would finish before they even started.

"Lisa—"

"Shhh," she said, touching him lightly with one finger, "it's all right."

She slid her other hand beneath him to cup his testicles, which were big and heavy. He had a much better body than the men her mother let her be with. He was younger, slimmer, stronger, and he smelled better.

"Mmmm," she said, leaning down to take him into her mouth.

"Oh, God, Lisa!" he moaned.

She tightened one hand around the base of his penis, using a technique her mother had taught her to keep a man from finishing too fast. It never occurred to him to wonder how she knew how to do this.

She slid her mouth up and down him wetly, her other hand roaming over his torso. He lifted his hips and groaned as she sucked him, but the music outside was too loud for anyone to hear him.

Lisa knew that if she let him come too soon he would be done for the night. She had to make him last, because she needed this. She released him from her mouth and lay down on her back next to him.

"Touch me," she said.

"Huh?"

"Come on," she said, "do what you want to me."

Danny Jennings couldn't believe his luck. His eyes had also adjusted to the darkness and he could make out the outline of her body. Her breasts were incredible, and he reached out and touched her gently, one hand on each. Her nipples were hard and he was fascinated by this.

"Squeeze them," she told him, "hard."

Danny was embarrassed because he was nineteen and had never been with a girl.

"Lisa," he said, "I never—"

"Shhh, baby," she said to him, "it's all right. We'll do it together. Come here."

She drew him to her, pressing their bodies together, and kissed him. He tasted so good because he wasn't an old man. She wondered if, after this, she'd be able to go back to having sex with older men to help her momma.

She had no idea that the excitement she was feeling now would soon turn to disappointment.

THIRTY-FIVE

Chance stopped by the back door and turned the knob. It wouldn't open. He tried pressing his shoulder to the door, but it wouldn't budge. He was going to need something to pry it open with. He would remember, after this, to always carry a knife with him.

He looked around and found a piece of wood. He jammed the end of it under the doorknob and then slammed his knee into the other end. The door popped open, the lock intact but the doorjamb splintered. Hopefully, the Barrows women would assume that someone had simply broken in to steal something.

He tossed aside the wood and entered the house.

Danny Jennings couldn't believe what was happening. Lisa Barrows was astride him, and he was buried deeply inside of her. He'd never felt anything like this in his life. It was amazing.

On the other hand, Lisa Barrows was disappointed. There was much more to sex than just jamming a man up inside of you, she was finding out. Danny Jennings didn't have the first inkling of what to do.

"Come on, come on!" she implored him.

"I—I don't know what you want . . ." he stammered.

"I want you to make me feel good."

Clumsily, he groped her breasts, but that didn't do anything for her either.

"Damn you, damn you!" she shouted in frustration.

The music was still loud outside and no one could hear her.

"Lisa . . ."

In a frenzy she began to bounce up and down on him. Again, to him this was ecstasy, but to her it was agony. He was not doing anything for her in return.

Her arms began to flail and her right hand struck something that was hanging on the wall, something metal. Her hand closed over it, and she grabbed it and raised it.

Danny Jennings's eyes were closed and he was about to explode. He did not see her bring the metal object down on his head. He felt only a flash of pain, and then nothing more as she continued to blindly strike out at him, again and again, blood spraying out over the hay, and all over her.

Moments later, when she realized what she had done, she screamed. . . .

As they were dancing Linda Barrows suddenly looked around her.

"What is it?" Clint asked.

"Did you hear something?"

"Only the music."

She listened intently for a moment, then shook her head.

"It was nothing, I guess."

"Let's keep dancing."

"What about my offer?" she asked. "A room, hot meals . . ."

"And?"

She shrugged.

"And who knows? Are you here with anyone?"

"No."

"I thought you were with a woman when I got here."

He shook his head.

"I just danced with her."

"Is there anyone . . . back home?"

"There is no back home," he said, "and if there was, there wouldn't be anyone there."

"No family?"

"No."

"No wife?"

"No wife, no parents, no brothers or sisters. I'm free as a bird."

"That's good," she said, touching the hair at the base of his neck with her hand, "that's very, very good."

Victoria was dancing with the fourth or fifth man who had asked her, but she was still watching Clint dance with the Barrows woman. Now she saw her rubbing the back of his neck and she felt more than a flash of jealousy.

She knew what Clint was trying to do. He was trying to gain the woman's confidence, but that didn't change the way she was feeling.

"You sure are a good dancer, miss," the man holding her said.

"Thank you . . ."

• • •

Chance stood just inside the kitchen and waited for his eyes to adjust to the darkness. He hoped Linda Barrows enjoyed dancing with Clint Adams and would continue to do it for a long time.

Once he could see he started to move around the house. The downstairs was the kitchen, the dining room, the living room, and what appeared to be an office. He spent most of the time in the office, but he didn't know what he was looking for. He'd just have to hope that he'd know what it was when he found it.

Lisa Barrows was lucky that when she killed Danny Jennings she was naked. She used his shirt—for he was naked, too—to wipe as much of his blood from her face, arms, and body as she could, and then put her dress back on.

She looked down at his body, his head all smashed in and bloody, and said, "I'm sorry, Danny. I guess I was wrong about young men. As usual, my momma was right."

She climbed down from the hayloft and, instead of going out the back way, back to the party, she went out the front and started to walk home.

Maybe Momma would understand.

"What's wrong?" Clint asked.

"I don't see my daughter."

She was looking around.

"Maybe she went off with a young man," Clint said. When he felt the woman stiffen in his arms, he knew he'd said something wrong.

"I hope not!" she said frostily.

"Maybe she's just dancing and you can't see her."

She stepped out of his arms and said, "I better go and look for her."

"But—"

"Where are you staying tonight?"

"I don't know."

"Come by the house," she said. "I'll have a room ready for you."

"Thanks—" he started to say, but she was gone.

Clint looked around, but he couldn't see Lisa either. He hoped the younger girl *had* gone off with Danny, and hadn't gone home.

With Linda gone, he looked around for Victoria.

THIRTY-SIX

Chance began to go through the desk and immediately he knew he'd found something. In a bottom drawer he found a bunch of men's wallets. He went through each one and found them empty. Why did Linda Barrows have so many men's wallets in her desk?

He was pondering that when he heard something. It took him a moment to realize that it was the front door opening. Someone was coming back.

Beneath the closed door of the office he saw a light. Someone was in the living room, and he could hear footsteps approaching the office. He looked around for an avenue of escape and saw a door on the right wall. He moved to it quickly, hoping it was not locked. When he turned the doorknob the door opened and he slipped inside, heaving a sigh of relief. Inside he almost fell before he realized he was standing at the top of a flight of stairs.

He regained his balance and watched the crack under

the door to see if a lamp was lit in the office. It was, and he wondered if he had closed the bottom drawer of the desk.

He held his breath, waiting for someone to come and open the door and take a look. He wondered if he should go down the stairs and see where they led. If it did open, though, it would be opened either by Linda or Lisa Barrows, neither of whom could threaten him physically, unless they had a weapon. He decided that if the door did open he'd just barrel over whoever opened it and get out of there. The worse they could do then was have him arrested for breaking into their house. If they did that, he'd just explain his theories to the sheriff and see what happened.

He could hear someone moving around the room and wondered what they were doing. Suddenly, the shadow of two feet became visible beneath the door, and he knew that someone was standing right in front of it. He held his breath and got ready to get out of there when suddenly he heard a click.

She'd locked the door.

He reached for the knob and tried to turn it, but it didn't budge.

He was locked in.

"Hey!" he shouted.

No answer. The shadows of the feet disappeared and he heard footsteps begin moving away.

"Hey, open up!" he called out.

The light went out.

"Hey!" he shouted, banging on the door with both hands. "Open this door."

He heard a woman's laughter, which faded as she apparently also closed the door to the office.

He banged on the door until his hands hurt too much to continue.

THIRTY-SEVEN

When Linda Barrows couldn't find Lisa she finally decided to go home and check and see if she was there. When she walked in, Lisa was sitting on the sofa in the living room, her feet drawn up to her chest. Linda immediately knew that going to the dance was a mistake.

"Lisa?"

Her daughter didn't look at her. Linda went and sat next to her.

"Lisa?"

Lisa took a sideways glance at her mother, then looked away. It was then that Linda noticed some red stains on her daughter's neck and in her hair.

"Lisa, what happened?"

Lisa gnawed on her thumbnail and then said, "I did a bad thing, Momma. A really bad thing."

Clint would have been careful about being seen with

Victoria, but he didn't see Linda or Lisa anywhere.

"Let's dance," he said, taking Victoria out onto the dance floor.

"That's all I've been doing," she complained, but she went willingly. "What's happened?" she asked.

"I don't know," Clint said. "Lisa disappeared, Linda went looking for her. I only hope they didn't go home."

"Why would they?"

"I don't know."

"What happened between you and Linda?"

"She invited me to her house."

"And you didn't go?"

"She invited me to come and be a guest." Clint relayed his conversation word for word—except for anything flirtatious that he or Linda might have said.

"That's all that was said?"

"Basically."

Victoria began to stroke the hair at the nape of Clint's neck and asked, "Even when she was doing this?"

Clint moved his head and said, "She was just trying to get me to come and stay at the boardinghouse."

"And what did you say?"

"I didn't answer yes or no," he said, "but I did tell her I had no place to stay tonight."

"And?"

"And she said she'd keep a room ready for me."

"Do you think you should go?"

"I think so," he said. "Chance might need help."

"Against two women?"

"Two women he thinks have been killing men."

"Well, what do you want to do?"

"I'd better go to the hotel, get my gear, and show up on her doorstep. Maybe by spending tonight there I can find something out."

"I'll go back to the hotel with you."

"No," Clint said, "you better stay here just in case one of them comes back."

"All right," she said reluctantly. She'd had enough of dancing for one night.

"And see if you can find Danny Jennings," Clint said. "Maybe he knows where Lisa went."

"I'll look around for him."

They stopped dancing and prepared to go their separate ways.

"Clint?"

"Yes?"

"Be careful," she said. "If those two women are killers . . ."

"I know," he said. "I'll be careful."

"Maybe," she said, "if they're killing men, I'm the one who should go and—"

"Never mind," Clint said. "Just stay here and find Danny Jennings."

She opened her mouth to protest, but he was too quick for her and was on his way.

THIRTY-EIGHT

"I'm sorry, Momma."

Linda cradled Lisa's head to her breast and patted her head.

"No, honey," she said, "I'm sorry. I never should have let you go. I knew that boy couldn't satisfy you. I just didn't know . . ."

She didn't know how her daughter would react. This was something Linda had not forseen, but she knew that she and Lisa were going to have to handle it.

"We have another problem to deal with," Linda said.

"What's that, Momma?"

"There might be a man coming tonight to stay."

"Oh, not tonight, Momma." Lisa raised her tear-streaked face to her mother.

"No, sweetie," Linda said, "not tonight. We'll let him stay here, that's all."

"Good."

"We'll have to be prepared for when they find young Jennings tomorrow morning, though."

"What will we do, Momma? People saw me with him."

"We'll just have to say that you came back here early, that's all."

"Can we prove it?"

"Don't worry, honey," Linda said. "I'll take care of everything. After all, it will only be Sheriff Cantwell asking questions."

"Momma?"

"Yes?"

Lisa wiped the tears from her face and sat up, looking at her mother.

"We have another problem."

"What's that?"

"I locked someone in the cellar."

"You what?"

Lisa nodded.

"When I came home someone was in the office, and he hid behind the cellar door. I locked it."

"Do you know who it was?"

Lisa shook her head.

"It was a man, though. He started yelling and pounding on the door when I locked it."

Well, here was something she could react to immediately.

"Let's go and see if we can find out who he is."

"Will we need a gun, Momma?" Lisa asked as they both got up.

"No, sweetie," Linda said. "We're not gonna open the door, and he can't kick it down because it's too heavy."

When Chance saw the light beneath the door again, he

decided to simply keep quiet and see what was going to happen next.

They went into the office and Linda lit the lamp on the desk. Both women walked to the door.

"Hello in there," Linda said.

No answer.

"Oh, come now," Linda said. "We know you're in there."

No answer.

Linda looked at Lisa.

"He's in there, Momma."

Linda signaled her daughter to be quiet.

"Maybe he went downstairs?" Lisa whispered.

Linda hoped not. If whoever it was went downstairs and found something, they wouldn't be able to let him out, ever. Right now maybe they just caught someone who was looking to steal something and thought he'd rob an empty house while the dance was going on.

"Do you want to tell us your name?"

No answer.

"Do you want us to send for the sheriff?"

A long pause and then a man's voice said, "I think that would be a good idea."

"Oh, you do, huh?" Linda asked. From the sound of the voice it was a young man. Could it be the same man who came to the door a few days ago looking for someone?

"Yes, I do."

"Well, maybe we will and maybe we won't. Do you want to tell us why you broke into our house?"

Another pause and then: "To rob you."

"Of what?"

"I don't know," the man said. "Whatever I could find."

"If I send for the sheriff he'll put you in jail."

"I didn't take anything."

"Only because we caught you."

"Then let me go," the man said, "and you'll never see me again."

"Did you damage anything?"

No answer.

"I think we'll look around a bit before we decide to let you go or not."

No reply.

"Can you breathe in there?"

"Yes."

"Don't fall down the steps."

"I won't."

"You might break your neck if you move around in the dark," Linda said. "I suggest you just sit on the top step and wait."

"All right," he said, after a moment.

Linda put her hand on the door and rubbed it in a circular motion.

"Don't go away."

She motioned for Lisa to follow her. She put the lamp out on the desk, and they left.

Chance listened intently with his ear to the door. He saw the light go out, and then heard them leave, closing the office door behind them. Taking Linda Barrows's advice he sat down on the top step.

He wondered if he should go down and see what was down there. What if they came back to let him out while he was down there? What if they came back with a weapon? His only chance to get out, in the face of a weapon, was to be ready to charge when the door opened. No, as curious as he was about what was down the stairs, his best bet was to stay right here and wait.

Wait for the women to let him out, or for Clint Adams to come and get him out.

THIRTY-NINE

Clint went back to the hotel, hoping to find Chance Monroe there. When he didn't he started to worry. What if both women had gone back to the house and caught him there? Would he have been able to use the force he needed to deal with them, despite the fact that they were women?

Clint went to his room to collect his saddlebags, and he decided to leave his rifle behind. No point in bringing an extra weapon that could end up being used against him.

"Checking out?" the clerk asked.

"As a matter of fact," Clint said, "I wasn't ever checked in."

It took five dollars to make sure that the clerk would swear to that, if asked.

He left the hotel and started walking to the boarding-house. He could hear from the music in the air that the dance behind the livery was still going on.

• • •

Linda examined the damage to her back door.

"Well, we'll have to get that fixed in the morning," she said. "For tonight we'll have to wedge the door shut with something."

"What are we gonna do about the man, Momma?" Lisa asked.

"We'll leave him locked up a little longer, Lisa, until I decide what to do with him."

"No," Lisa said, "I meant about the man who's coming here tonight."

"Well, first of all, he might not come," Linda said, wedging a chair up against the door. "And if he does, we'll just give him a room. In fact, why don't you go and get one ready, just in case."

"What about Danny?"

"Did you love that boy, Lisa?"

"No."

"Then don't worry about it."

"But he's dead, Momma."

"I know he is, sweetie—and now that you remind me, when you go upstairs wash that blood off of yourself, and make sure you do a good job."

"Yes, Momma."

"If that man does show up, I don't want him wondering what's going on. Understand?"

"Yes, Momma. What if the man we have locked up makes noise?"

"I don't think it can be heard upstairs," Linda said, "but maybe I should see to it."

"Do you need help?"

"No, Lisa, I don't," Linda said. "You go and do what I told you, now. I'll handle things down here."

"Yes, Momma."

When Lisa was gone Linda shook her head, made sure the back door was held tightly closed, and left the kitchen.

Victoria was worried. Neither Linda nor Lisa Barrows were in evidence, and neither were Chance Monroe nor Danny Jennings. Clint wasn't there, either. She was the only one of the players in this drama who was at the dance.

She was about to leave when she heard somebody call her name.

Chance almost fell asleep and toppled off the top step. Some detective, he thought. Would Talbot Roper be dozing off at a time like this? Not likely.

Suddenly, he heard someone enter the office and the lamp was lit again. He scrambled to his feet and got himself ready, just in case that someone was going to open the door.

Linda Barrows knew what would happen when she opened the door, and she was ready for it. She had a large tree branch in her hand, the width of a man's arm, that she had smoothed down with a knife into an effective club. She had a gun in the house, but she had never yet had to use it.

She held the club in one hand, unlocked the door with the other, and then stepped back. As she had suspected, as soon as she unlocked the door the man swung it open and charged out. She knew he planned to run right over her, but instead she sidestepped and swung the club with both hands. She caught Chance Monroe right in the belly, driving all the air out of him. She then jabbed the end of the club into his stomach and pushed with all her strength. Chance had no choice but to backpedal through the door again. He was going too fast, though, thanks to Linda's push, and he stepped right off the top step and went tumbling down to the bottom, where he lay motionless.

Linda didn't bother to go down and check on him. She simply swung the door shut again and locked it. If he wasn't dead, that would at least keep him quiet for a while.

Just as she locked the door she heard a knock at the front door.

Excellent timing.

FORTY

When Linda Barrows opened the door, Clint smiled at her and dangled his saddlebags.

"I decided to take you up on your offer."

Poised, Linda smiled back and said, "Good. True to my word I have a room ready. Come in."

She led him into the living room. If the man at the bottom of the steps woke up now and made noise, Clint would hear him. The club she had used on the man was hidden just beneath the sofa, if she needed it.

In the split second before she had shoved the man back through the door and down the stairs she had not been able to get a good enough look at him to recognize him. She still did not know if he was someone she had seen before.

"My daughter is upstairs, putting the finishing touches on your room. Just let me call up to her—"

159

"Why don't you go on up," Clint suggested. "I'll just have a seat and wait here."

He watched Linda Barrows's reaction. She didn't want to go upstairs.

"Uh . . . I think I'll just call out to her. She'll hear me, and there's no one else in the house to wake up."

It was obvious to Clint that she didn't want to leave him alone downstairs.

"Fine," he said.

Linda walked to the stairs and called up, "Lisa? Come down, our guest is here."

It took only a few seconds and then Lisa Barrows came down. Clint noticed that her hair was wet.

"This is Clint . . ." Linda said, giving him a chance to supply a last name, but he didn't. "He's our guest. Is his room ready?"

"Yes, Momma," Lisa said. She frowned at Clint and asked, "Didn't I see you at the dance?"

"Yes, I was there," Clint said. "I got to town today and heard about it. I thought it might be fun. I ended up dancing with a very lovely woman."

"Thank you, sir," Linda said.

Clint decided to try something.

"But didn't I see you with a young man?"

Lisa looked quickly at Linda.

"That was Danny Jennings," Linda said. "They had one dance together, and then Danny suddenly disappeared—didn't he, Lisa?"

"Yes, Momma."

"I think Danny might have gone off with another girl who would give him what he wanted . . . if you get my meaning?"

"Oh, I get it," Clint said.

"Lisa, would you show Mr. . . . uh, Clint to his room, please?"

"Yes, Momma."

"Breakfast will be at nine a.m., Clint, if that's all right?"

"That's fine."

"Good. Lisa?"

"This way . . . Clint."

Clint followed Lisa up the stairs, enjoying the view of her tight little butt despite the possibility that she might be a killer—if Chance Monroe was right, of course.

Victoria turned and saw Ida approaching her. She was a little surprised to see a whorehouse madam at this dance.

"Yes?"

"That is your name, isn't it?" Ida asked. "Victoria?"

"That's right."

"I was looking for Mr. Adams."

"He's not here right now," Victoria said. "Did you find something out about my husband?"

"I did, but I don't know—"

"Come on, you can tell me."

"Are you sure?"

"Yes."

"He did show up at one of my competitors," she said. "He went upstairs with one of the girls and . . . conducted business, and then he asked where a good place to stay was. Apparently, he didn't want to stay in a hotel."

"Probably didn't want to sign a register," Victoria said. "So, where did he go?"

"He went to the boardinghouse that Linda Barrows runs. At least, he was told about the place. Whether he actually went there or not nobody knows. I'm sorry."

"There's no need to be," Victoria said, "you've been very helpful. Thank you."

If Henry did go to the Barrows Boardinghouse, then maybe Chance Monroe was right about those women. She had to find Clint and tell him, even if it meant going to the house herself.

Again, she turned to leave, and then someone started yelling something about somebody being dead.

FORTY-ONE

Danny Jennings had been found because another couple had decided to go into the livery stable and use the hayloft. When the girl saw Danny's body she started to scream, and then so did the boy. That brought people running—including Sheriff Cantwell.

"Anybody know who the last person with Danny Jennings was?" he asked.

"I do," Victoria said.

"Ma'am?"

"It was Lisa Barrows."

A murmur went up from the crowd that had gathered outside the stable. All the music had stopped, and the party was now over. Danny Jennings's mother—a widow—had been taken to her home in hysterics by neighbors.

"Are you going to go and question Lisa and her mother, Sheriff?" Victoria asked.

"Well . . ."

"You have to, Sheriff," someone else said.

"She was the last one with him," a third person said, and then the crowd started calling for the sheriff to take some action.

"Look, all of you calm down and go home. I'll look into this," the sheriff said.

He had his two deputies go through the crowd, trying to persuade people to go home.

"When will you be speaking to the Barrowses?" Victoria asked.

Cantwell looked at her and then said, "Ma'am, you don't even live in this town—"

"I can still be concerned about murder, Sheriff."

"I'll be talking to them tonight," Cantwell said, "as soon as I get the boy's body taken care of. Is that satisfactory?"

"That's fine," Victoria said. Then she added to herself, By that time I will have been there already.

She left the livery and headed for the Barrows Boardinghouse.

Lisa Barrows showed Clint to his room, which was spacious and comfortable.

"My mother and I have rooms at the other end of the house on this floor."

That was good, Clint thought. He wouldn't have to pass their rooms to go downstairs after they'd gone to sleep.

"Do you turn in early?" Clint asked.

"That depends," Lisa said, but she didn't say on what. Then she said, "I think we will tonight, though. It's been a tiring day."

"Well, good night, then," Clint said. "See you at breakfast."

"Good night, Mr. . . . uh, Clint."

She backed out of the room and closed the door. Clint put his saddlebags on the bed—a much better bed than he had at the hotel—and walked to the door to listen. He opened the door a crack and was able to see the stairway from where he was. He just caught her back as she was going down.

He closed the door and took a deep breath. He was now stuck in his room until he saw them go to bed. That meant he was going to have to stand at his door watching for who knew how long.

He wondered what was happening at the dance. He wondered where Chance Monroe was. Had he gotten out of the house before the women got home, or was he somewhere in the house? And what was Victoria doing?

He cracked the door again, tried to find a comfortable position, and resigned himself to standing there for a long while.

The first thing that struck Chance was the pain. He couldn't move his right arm without causing lots of pain. He lay still for a while after he awoke, trying to reconstruct the circumstances that had led to his present situation.

She'd pushed him down the stairs!

That bitch! She was waiting for him to do just what he did, and *she* surprised *him*.

He tried his left arm and found that he could move that one. He got it beneath him and pushed himself to a seated position. He felt a pain in his back, but he thought that was probably a bruise, maybe a sprain of some kind. He tried his legs, and they were working. The right arm, though, was broken. He was sure of that. He cradled it to his side, where he would try to keep it out of harm's way.

Okay, he was in the dark at the bottom of the stairs. He no longer thought they might open the door and let him go. That meant he might as well investigate his surroundings, just to see where he was.

He had some lucifer matches in his pocket, and dug one out to strike it. When he did he saw by the small flame that he was in some kind of a root cellar. The floor was dirt, and there were some shelves against the wall, but otherwise the cellar seemed pretty empty.

Except for some odd humps in the floor. There were about a dozen of them spread out around the room. He got painfully to his feet—yup, his back was probably sprained—and shuffled over to one of the humps in the floor. The match went out and he lit another, but he didn't think he needed it to figure out what the hump was.

It looked to him like there were twelve graves in that floor, and it didn't take a genius to figure out what the empty wallets and graves meant.

"What do we do now, Momma?" Lisa asked. "We got one man in the cellar and another one upstairs."

"We're going to have to make sure the man in the cellar doesn't make any noise," Linda said.

"You said he couldn't be heard upstairs."

"I want to play it safe, Lisa," Linda said. "We have an unusual situation here, and we have to deal with it."

"What will you do to him?"

"We'll take the gun along," Linda said.

"We can't fire a gun without the man upstairs hearing it."

"The man downstairs doesn't know that," Linda said. "You'll hold the gun on him while I tie him up and gag him. Once that's done we can get some sleep. In the morning we'll have a fresh outlook on things.''

"All right, Momma.''

"Let's go," Linda said. "He might be dead anyway, from the fall.''

FORTY-TWO

Clint decided he should probably be a little bolder. If Chance was still in the house, maybe even a captive, would the women just go to sleep? He figured he could be waiting up here for them for hours while they were doing something downstairs.

He decided he'd better go and see what they were doing. After all, even if he was caught, they were two women and he was armed.

He slipped from the room and down the hall to the head of the stairs. He was just in time to hear Linda say, "Let's go to the office."

He waited a few beats, then quietly came down the stairs. He saw an open door and a light burning inside the room. There was also some movement in the room. He came down the rest of the way and moved quietly to the door so he could peer in.

Linda Barrows had just taken a gun from her desk and handed it to Lisa.

"Just hold it on him while I tie him up . . . if he's still alive," she said.

"Yes, Momma."

They had to be talking about Chance, but where was he?

He watched them move to another door in the room, and Linda unlocked it. When she opened it, it was pitch-black inside.

"We'll need a lamp, or we'll fall down the steps."

She went back to the desk and took the lamp from there. There was another burning on the wall, right near the door Clint was standing at.

"All right, follow me," Linda said.

At that moment there was a knock on the front door and both women—and Clint—froze.

"Who's that?" Lisa asked.

The knock was repeated.

"I don't know," Linda said, "but we're going to have to find out."

She closed the door and locked it again, then hurried to the desk and put the lamp back.

"Come on," she said to Lisa.

"Oh, Momma, what if they found Danny?" Lisa asked.

Found Danny? Clint thought. What had she done to Danny?

"You better bring the gun, Lisa," Linda said, "just in case . . ."

Clint moved quickly, getting away from the door and hiding behind the sofa. Linda and Lisa left the living room to go down the hall to the front door. As curious as he was about who was at the door, he had to get into the office and see what was behind that door.

He hurried to the office and entered, leaving the door open. He moved immediately to the other door, unlocked it, and opened it.

"Chance?"

There was a long moment of silence and then he heard Chance call out in a whisper, "Clint? Is that you?"

"It's me. Come on, get up here."

"I can't," Chance said. "I've got a broken arm and a sprained back. I need help."

"All right," Clint said, "I'm coming."

The light from behind him lit the steps, but he couldn't see what was at the bottom of them. He hurried down to bring Chance up before the women returned.

"Where are they?" Chance asked.

"Front door. What happened?"

"That bitch pushed me down the stairs!"

"The mother?"

"Yes."

Clint looked around, but it was dark.

"What's down here?"

"It's some kind of root cellar," Chance said, "but there's more than roots down here."

"Like what?"

"Graves," Chance said. "Lots of them."

"You mean . . . they killed the men and then buried them down here?"

"That's right."

"Is Henry Williams here?"

"I don't know, but there are a bunch of wallets in the bottom drawer of that desk up there. Maybe his is among them."

"That'll be for Victoria to discover," Clint said. "Let's get you out of here and go and get the sheriff."

He helped Chance to his feet. Since Chance's right arm

was broken, Clint had to put his left around his neck. That meant that Chance's hip was right against Clint's right hip, and gun.

"Let's go," Clint said.

Clint started up the steps and stopped when he saw Linda Barrows at the head of them, pointing a gun at him and Chance.

"You disappoint me, Clint."

"I'm taking him out of here, Linda."

"I don't think so."

"Who was at the door?" he asked.

"Somebody you'll be interested to see."

She stepped aside just enough so that he could see Victoria, who had one arm held behind her by Lisa. Clint felt that Victoria probably could have gotten free from Lisa, if it wasn't for the gun Linda was holding.

"Let her go, Linda."

"I thought you didn't know her." Linda asked. "I thought you just danced with her."

"Let her go," he said again. "She's got nothing to do with this."

"Take your gun out, Clint, with your left hand, and toss it up here."

"I don't think I can do that, Linda."

"Why not?"

"You'll shoot me once I'm unarmed."

Linda pressed the gun to Victoria's temple.

"I'll shoot her if you don't," she said. "Make your choice."

It didn't take Clint long to make up his mind.

"Okay, take it easy," Clint said. "I've got to let him down first."

"If you try anything, I'll shoot you, and then her."

"And then him?" Clint asked, lowering Chance into a

seated position on one of the steps. "And then what, Linda? Are you going to bury us down here, too?"

"Toss your gun up!"

"How many people are you going to kill?"

"Clint," Victoria called out, "Lisa killed Danny Jennings."

That surprised Clint.

"Now why would she do that, Linda?" he asked. "Danny didn't have any money."

"It was an accident," Linda said. "Now stop talking and toss up your gun!"

"Okay, here it comes," Clint said. He reached for it left-handed, drew it out, and tossed it up the steps. It didn't reach her. Instead, it struck the second step from the top, then fell down a couple more before it stopped. It was out of his reach, but out of hers, as well.

"Sorry," Clint said. "Can we come up now?"

"No," Linda said, "stay there."

"What are we gonna do, Momma?" Lisa asked.

"Just give me a minute, honey."

"The sheriff's on his way over," Victoria said. "Lisa was the last one seen with the Jennings boy. You better think of something fast."

"Shut up!"

"She's right, Linda," Clint said. "You better think fast."

"Shut up, shut up," Linda said. "I'll kill you all now."

Suddenly, Clint felt something slide into his hand. It was a small gun of some kind, a derringer from the feel of it. Chance had slipped it to him.

"Come on, Linda," Clint said, taunting the woman now. "Show your daughter how smart you are when you don't have time to plan people's deaths."

"Momma?" Lisa asked. "What do we do?"

On cue Victoria also urged, "Yes, Linda, come on, make a decision."

Clint could see from the look on Linda's face that she was about to come apart. She and Lisa must have been killing men for months, maybe years. Lisa must have been learning things from her mother that no other mother had taught her daughter. The look on Lisa's face as she stared at her mother told him a lot about her, too. Her eyes were totally blank as she waited for her mother to say or do something that would save them.

Suddenly, they all heard a pounding on the front door.

"Oops," Clint said, "that's the sheriff. Time to make a decision."

And he raised the derringer.

FORTY-THREE

It was odd. In all the years he'd been using a gun he didn't remember ever being outshot by a woman. Actually, she didn't really outshoot him. She must have made up her mind to fire even before the pounding on the door. In any case she fired a split second before he did. Her bullet was wide and to the left, and tugged at the sleeve of his shirt and creased his arm. His bullet was fired more truly. It struck her between the breasts. The bullet was so small you almost couldn't see where it struck her, but then the blood started to seep into the front of her shirt.

Even though his shot was the fatal one, he wondered if he felt more pain than she did, from the larger caliber.

"Momma!" Lisa shouted.

The bullet that struck him drove him off balance, and Lisa reacted much faster than he would have expected.

When his bullet struck Linda, she released her gun and

174

it fell all the way down the steps, so while he was off balance Clint also had to duck the gun.

Lisa, seeing her mother shot, instantly started down the steps, but she wasn't after her mother's gun, she was after Clint's.

"Clint—" Chance called, seeing what she was doing.

"Damn!" Clint shouted. "Don't, Lisa!"

She was beyond hearing. She bent over and reached for his gun.

Clint had killed one woman already, but that didn't make it any easier. As if sensing this, Victoria came down the stairs behind Lisa, put her foot against her butt, and pushed. The girl sprang off the step and flew through the air at Clint, who ducked. She sailed past him, barely missed hitting Chance with her legs, and landed at the base of the steps in a crumpled heap.

Clint looked up at Victoria, who was standing with her hands over her mouth.

"I didn't mean—" she said.

"I know." He went to the base of the steps to check on Lisa. She was lying with her head at an odd angle, dead from a broken neck.

"Could have happened to me," Chance said, looking down at her.

"Yeah," Clint said. "Come on, let's get out of here."

He helped Chance to his feet and up the stairs. At the top Victoria took Chance from him while he checked Linda. His bullet had flown true and she was dead.

"Damn!" he said.

"You had no choice," Victoria said.

The pounding on the front door was still going on.

"Victoria, go and see who that is."

"Probably the sheriff," she said. "I had to shame him into coming here after they found Danny Jennings. Lisa . . . beat him to death with something . . . a branding iron,

I think.''

    ''Well, then,'' Clint said, ''I won't worry about killing
Linda if you don't worry about killing Lisa.''

    ''It's a deal,'' she said, and went to let Sheriff Cantwell
in.

FORTY-FOUR

Victoria Williams identified one of the wallets in Linda Barrows's desk as her husband's.

"Are you sure?" Sheriff Cantwell asked.

"I gave it to him."

"Well, I guess that's it, then," Cantwell said. "That and those graves in the basement."

They were in Cantwell's office the next morning, trying to tie up all the loose ends.

"Are you going to dig any of them up?" Clint asked.

"What for? Can't identify them. There ain't nothing in the wallets, and there ain't gonna be nothin' on them. They wouldn't be that stupid."

Clint wanted to point out that the women were stupid enough to bury the dead men in their basement, but he decided against it. He actually didn't want the sheriff digging around down there.

Cantwell looked over at Chance Monroe, whose arm was in a sling.

"Guess you was right, Mr. Monroe. You must be a pretty good detective."

"He is," Victoria said.

"Anything to keep us from leaving town, Sheriff?" Clint asked.

"Nothin' at all."

In fact, Cantwell was going to be glad to see them all go.

"Come on," Clint said, and led Victoria and Chance outside.

"Where are you off to?" Chance asked.

"I'm going to see Victoria back to Dalton, where she can get a stagecoach. What about you?"

"Well, if you don't mind," Chance said, "I'll go to Denver and try to meet Mr. Talbot Roper. I think I could learn a lot from him about being a detective."

"I think you could, too," Clint said, "and he could probably put that extra sense to good use. I'll send him a telegram and let him know you're coming."

"Thanks, Clint!"

They shook hands and Chance went off to pack his things, limping because of his sprained back.

"Well," Victoria said, "I found Henry, didn't I?"

"If he's in one of those graves," Clint said.

"You think he is, don't you?"

"I think so, yeah," Clint said. "Do you want to dig him up to make sure?"

"No," Victoria said. "I'm satisfied that he's down there. I just wonder what happened to the money."

"I have a theory about that."

"What is it?"

"Sheriff Cantwell said that the Barrows women did not have any money in the bank."

"So?"

"So, when the sheriff arrived last night and we went down to that cellar with a lamp I noticed that all the mounds in the floor were the same size, except one. It was smaller, and it looked fresh, as if they dug it up now and then."

Her eyes widened.

"You mean—"

"Yep," he said. "They put the money they stole in the ground."

Victoria looked around.

"Do you think the sheriff would mind—"

"What he doesn't know won't hurt him," Clint said. "I thought I saw a shovel down there, too."

"What are we waiting for?"

Watch for

WILD BULL

178th in the bold GUNSMITH series
from Jove

Coming in October!

J. R. ROBERTS

THE
GUNSMITH

__THE GUNSMITH #156: DAKOTA GUNS	0-515-11507-X/$3.99	
__THE GUNSMITH #157: SEMINOLE VENGEANCE	0-515-11530-4/$3.99	
__THE GUNSMITH #158: THE RANSOM	0-515-11553-3/$3.99	
__THE GUNSMITH #159: THE HUNTSVILLE TRIP	0-515-11571-1/$3.99	
__THE GUNSMITH #160: THE TEN YEAR HUNT	0-515-11593-2/$3.99	
__THE GUNSMITH #162: THE LAST GREAT SCOUT	0-515-11635-1/$3.99	
__THE GUNSMITH #163: THE WILD WOMEN OF	0-515-11656-4/$3.99	
GLITTER GULCH		
__THE GUNSMITH #164: THE OMAHA HEAT	0-515-11688-2/$3.99	
__THE GUNSMITH #165: THE DENVER RIPPER	0-515-11703-X/$3.99	
__THE GUNSMITH #167: CHINAVILLE	0-515-11747-1/$4.50	
__THE GUNSMITH #168: THE FRENCH MODELS	0-515-11767-6/$4.50	
__THE GUNSMITH #170: THE ELLIOTT BAY	0-515-11918-0/$4.50	
MURDERS		
__THE GUNSMITH #172: THE HANGING WOMAN	0-515-11844-3/$4.99	
__THE GUNSMITH #173: JERSEY LILY	0-515-11862-1/$4.99	
__THE GUNSMITH #174: GUNQUICK	0-515-11880-X/$4.99	
__THE GUNSMITH #175: GRAVE HUNT	0-515-11896-6/$4.99	
__THE GUNSMITH #176: TRIPLE CROSS	0-515-11926-1/$4.99	
__THE GUNSMITH #177: BURIED PLEASURES	0-515-11943-1/$4.99	
__THE GUNSMITH #178: WILD BULL (10/96)	0-515-11957-1/$4.99	

Payable in U.S. funds. No cash orders accepted. Postage & handling: $1.75 for one book, 75¢ for each additional. Maximum postage $5.50. Prices, postage and handling charges may change without notice. Visa, Amex, MasterCard call 1-800-788-6262, ext. 1, refer to ad # 206g

Or, check above books	Bill my: ☐ Visa ☐ MasterCard ☐ Amex	
and send this order form to:		(expires)
The Berkley Publishing Group	Card#_____	
390 Murray Hill Pkwy., Dept. B		($15 minimum)
East Rutherford, NJ 07073	Signature_____	
Please allow 6 weeks for delivery.	Or enclosed is my: ☐ check ☐ money order	
Name_____	Book Total	$_____
Address_____	Postage & Handling	$_____
City_____	Applicable Sales Tax	$_____
	(NY, NJ, PA, CA, GST Can.)	
State/ZIP_____	Total Amount Due	$_____

*If you enjoyed this book,
subscribe now and get...*

TWO FREE

A $7.00 VALUE–

If you would like to read more
of the very best, most exciting,
adventurous, action-packed
Westerns being published
today, you'll want to subscribe
to True Value's Western Home
Subscription Service.

Each month the editors of True
Value will select the 6 very best
Westerns from America's leading publishers for special
readers like you. You'll be able
to preview these new titles as
soon as they are published,
FREE for ten days with no
obligation!

TWO FREE BOOKS

When you subscribe, we'll send
you your first month's shipment
of the newest and best 6 Westerns for you to preview. With
your first shipment, two of these
books will be yours as our intro-
ductory gift to you absolutely
FREE (a $7.00 value), regard-
less of what you decide to do. If

you like them, as much as we
think you will, keep all six books
but pay for just 4 at the low subscriber rate of just $2.75 each. If
you decide to return them, keep
2 of the titles as our gift. No
obligation.

Special Subscriber Savings

When you become a True Value
subscriber you'll save money
several ways. First, all regular
monthly selections will be billed
at the low subscriber price of
just $2.75 each. That's at least a
savings of $4.50 each month
below the publishers price. Second, there is never any shipping,
handling or other hidden
charges—*Free home delivery*.
What's more there is no minimum number of books you must
buy, you may return any selec-
tion for full credit and you can
cancel your subscription at any
time. A TRUE VALUE!

A special offer for people who enjoy reading the best Westerns published today.

WESTERNS!

NO OBLIGATION

Mail the coupon below

To start your subscription and receive 2 FREE WESTERNS, fill out the coupon below and mail it today. We'll send your first shipment which includes 2 FREE BOOKS as soon as we receive it.

Mail To: **True Value Home Subscription Services, Inc. P.O. Box 5235 120 Brighton Road, Clifton, New Jersey 07015-5235**

YES! I want to start reviewing the very best Westerns being published today. Send me my first shipment of 6 Westerns for me to preview FREE for 10 days. If I decide to keep them, I'll pay for just 4 of the books at the low subscriber price of $2.75 each; a total $11.00 (a $21.00 value). Then each month I'll receive the 6 newest and best Westerns to preview Free for 10 days. If I'm not satisfied I may return them within 10 days and owe nothing. Otherwise I'll be billed at the special low subscriber rate of $2.75 each; a total of $16.50 (at least a $21.00 value) and save $4.50 off the publishers price. There are never any shipping, handling or other hidden charges. I understand I am under no obligation to purchase any number of books and I can cancel my subscription at any time, no questions asked. In any case the 2 FREE books are mine to keep.

Name _____

Street Address _____ Apt. No. _____

City _____ State _____ Zip Code _____

Telephone _____

Signature _____
(if under 18 parent or guardian must sign)

Terms and prices subject to change. Orders subject
to acceptance by True Value Home Subscription
Services. Inc.

11943-1

Darnell Baynes took his three sons
from their Louisiana farm and the carnage
of the Civil War out to the rugged Montana
Territory. He taught them to shoot fast,
work hard, and always treat a lady with
respect. But surviving on the frontier
is a long, lonely battle.

THE
BAYNES
CLAN

by JOHN S. McCORD

__NEVADA TOUGH   0-425-14982-X/$4.99
Darnell Baynes is tall in the saddle once again, riding to
Nevada for the good of the family. Someone is stealing
gold from the Baynes Clan—and they're about to find out
that this old dog still knows a few nasty tricks.

__CALIFORNIA EAGLES   0-515-11725-0/$4.99
__WYOMING GIANT   0-515-11651-3/$4.99
__TEXAS COMEBACKER   0-515-11585-1/$4.99
__MONTANA HORSEMAN   0-515-11532-0/$4.99

Payable in U.S. funds. No cash orders accepted. Postage & handling: $1.75 for one book, 75¢
for each additional. Maximum postage $5.50. Prices, postage and handling charges may
change without notice. Visa, Amex, MasterCard call 1-800-788-6262, ext. 1, refer to ad # 511b*

Or, check above books   Bill my: ☐ Visa ☐ MasterCard ☐ Amex
and send this order form to: (expires)
The Berkley Publishing Group   Card#_____
390 Murray Hill Pkwy., Dept. B   ($15 minimum)
East Rutherford, NJ 07073   Signature_____
Please allow 6 weeks for delivery.   Or enclosed is my: ☐ check ☐ money order
Name_____   Book Total $_____
Address_____   Postage & Handling $_____
City_____   Applicable Sales Tax $_____
                                        (NY, NJ, PA, CA, GST Can.)
State/ZIP_____   Total Amount Due $_____